The Hit-and-Run Man

The Hit-and-Run Man

Derrick R. Bickley

Chapter One

Greenfield hardly noticed the icy drizzle biting into his face, aware of nothing but the shadowy figure ahead of him. His hand was sweaty, uncannily so in the freezing cold of the night, as it closed around the butt of the automatic pistol in his pocket. In a matter of minutes the man who walked some thirty yards ahead of him along the wet, near-deserted streets would be dead. The nightmare would be over.

Out of Hopdale Avenue and into School Road, Greenfield closed up slightly on his quarry. Never having fired a gun before, he knew he had to get close to be sure of hitting the target, but he wanted to close the gap gradually, avoiding arousing the suspicions of the man ahead.

Greenfield couldn't believe he was thinking like this. He wasn't a criminal. Even now the thought that he was about to kill a man seemed unreal, a ghastly dream. How did he allow himself to get into this mess? What was an honest, respectable member of the community doing out on the streets with a gun, on a freezing December night, following a man he was about to blow to Kingdom come? It was crazy.

The time was almost here. Soon the cramped, terraced houses would give way to the empty school buildings. On the other side of the road would be the school's playing fields, dark and deserted. This was where it was to happen.

Greenfield thought of Pauline and his daughter, Diane. That was where he should be, at home with them, warm and contented, not out on the icy cold streets, a gun in his pocket, stalking the man he had to kill.

He wondered what Pauline was doing at that moment. Diane tucked up in bed, she was probably relaxing with a cup of coffee, watching a film on television perhaps, or reading her favourite magazine. In fact, nothing could have been further from the truth.

Their parting a couple of days before had been far from pleasant, but he couldn't see what else he could have done or said. How can you tell your wife that you have to go away for a few days to murder someone? His inability to offer an acceptable explanation for his leaving home for a short while had done nothing to allay her suspicions that he was running to another woman. He supposed it was the obvious thing to suspect. Surely, she could know nothing of the night in Barcelona. How much had her fears preyed on her mind since he had been gone? Could she really think he had left her for good? Oh, how he wished he could be there with her at this moment, to hold her hand, take her in his arms, reassure her.

The man ahead paused momentarily, pulling the collar of his coat up around his ears. It crossed Greenfield's mind that this would almost certainly be the last conscious act of this man's life. Not much of a final contribution. Yet Greenfield knew he would never forget it. He would see it by night, by day, wherever he was going, whatever he was doing. This man's last deliberate act before Greenfield squeezed the trigger and brought his life to a bloody conclusion.

A thousand times over the past three months Greenfield has asked himself how he could have been so stupid, without finding an answer. Tonight was no exception. The male ego, that can push a man to such great heights, can so often be his downfall. He could still see now the first fleeting flash of those big, blue eyes and remember the sensation that instantly stirred within him.

Memories of that warm summer night in Barcelona came back to haunt him once more, swirling around his brain with thoughts of Pauline, his daughter, his home and the man he had to kill. Silent tears ran down his cheeks as the icy rain turned to snow.

He was suddenly aware that the houses had disappeared, the dark, empty school buildings looming beside him. Across the road it was impossible to see even the outline of a soccer goalpost in the light of the old, inadequate street lamps.

Greenfield closed up quickly on his quarry. Speed was everything now. His hand tightened on the pistol in his pocket, already primed for firing, his finger now on the trigger.

There could be no hesitating. The time had come. It was the only way to end the nightmare that had begun three months before at the start of a business trip to Spain.

He knew he must not fail.

Chapter Two

Howard Greenfield had never got used to flying. Waiting in the airport departure lounge after check-in, there was always a twinge of apprehension. The obvious increased security around London and in Heathrow following the recent I.R.A. bomb attack on the Stock Exchange certainly wasn't helping that either. He wasn't sure what made him more nervous; the possibility of being caught up in an I.R.A. blast or police officers carrying sub-machine guns. Even so, he enjoyed his trips abroad, an undeniably worthwhile perk of his job.

He felt no guilt in taking pleasure in such perks, having worked his way up from the bottom to the top by virtue of his own efforts. Joining Impact Publicity Services Ltd., one of London's leading firms in the field of advertising and public relations, shortly after leaving school, as a voucher clerk and general dogsbody, spending hours mindlessly cutting out copies of clients' advertisements from the seemingly endless supply of magazines and newspapers that poured into the office, he worked his way up to Senior Account Executive, with special responsibility for overseas accounts. It had meant years of fetching and carrying, hard work and dedication. Now, approaching his forty-third birthday, there was only one step left to make. When Jason Henderson finally decided to retire, he hoped to be a leading contender for the Managing Directorship.

As he had never regarded himself as particularly good looking, Greenfield had always considered it something of a miracle that he had managed to attract a girl like Pauline. That day she first appeared in the typing pool at Impact Publicity is one he would never forget. Only a few days past her twenty-second birthday, she was slim, quite tall, only a couple of inches shorter than he was, with a pretty, round face and long, black hair that hung down her back almost to the waist. Every time she had come near him, in the same room even, he had wanted to reach out and run his fingers through her long, flowing hair.

Always uncomfortable around the female sex, he had spent his younger manhood years immersed in his work. While other men his age were chatting up and dating girls, he had eyes only for Impact Publicity, busily climbing the career ladder. So, at the age of twenty-seven, he found himself still totally inexperienced with women.

The arrival of Pauline in the typing pool had a new and profound effect on him. Because of his discomfort and inexperience, he had tended to shut out the opposite sex, building a mental barrier, but with Pauline this had become impossible to maintain after the first meeting. At work he found it difficult to keep his eyes off her, made excuses to be near her, brushed by her so closely there was just the slightest contact, while at home he lay for hours on his bed, staring at the ceiling, just thinking about her.

His awkwardness made the process of getting to know her a slow one. So it was months before he built up enough courage to ask her out, only managing it then, much to his embarrassment, with a deep reddening of his cheeks. He was staggered when she instantly agreed.

With his shyness and lack of experience making the early dates near disasters, he always expected her to refuse the next offer. To his surprise, she never did.

Greenfield was never able to fathom his appeal. He felt he looked older than his years, his hair already showing signs of thinning on top. With a body that was thin and looked under-developed compared with most men his age, despite a more than reasonable appetite, he had always seen himself as unattractive, his former total disinterest in the opposite sex possibly a subconscious dread of having these feelings confirmed. No man lives happily with rejection.

Pauline, though, seemed to like him and the shy awkwardness slowly faded as the relationship blossomed. They first made love in her parents' caravan, a weekend retreat set deep in the Kentish countryside. She had told her parents she was going with a girl friend. He had gone with mixed feelings of hope, anticipation, but mostly apprehension. She had aroused in him feelings and longings he had never known before and he was desperate to make love to her, but this brought a new worry all of its own.

He didn't want her to know that at the age of twenty-seven this would be his first time. Pauline had told him she was not a virgin and he had led her to believe he wasn't either. Determined as he was to maintain that impression, his resolve crumbled as he looked on a naked woman for the first time. It was impossible to hide the sharp intake of breath or control the spellbound stare of his eyes as they joyously took in every detail of the vision before him. His hands trembled as he undressed.

Concerned that his ignorance of what to do would show him up proved unfounded. Once in bed with the girl he loved so dearly and wanted so desperately, everything seemed to happen so naturally. Pauline gave no indication then, nor had she since, that she was aware that on that rainy Sunday afternoon she was bringing Howard Greenfield's virginity to an overdue end.

A few months later, shortly after his twenty-eighth birthday, they were married, but his vision of night after night of hectic sexual activity, making up for his lost years, took a nasty jolt when she became pregnant after only three months. Someone once told him that the world's best contraceptive was a young child in the house and this he found to be undoubtedly true.

Even so, as he waited for his flight to be called, he felt he had little to complain about, entering middle-age with a degree of contentment many would envy. He had a good home, a caring wife whose looks made nonsense of her years, a daughter who was his pride and joy and a career that still had a challenge to offer, still presented a final pinnacle to climb.

So why did the first, accidental, contact with those large, blue eyes, across a crowded airport departure lounge, arouse such a stirring within him? It was only a fleeting instant, a moment's hesitancy as her eyes met his, before she lowered them, uncertainly, appearing coyly conscious of his stare.

Greenfield felt he should look away, but was unable to. She was beautiful in an almost bewitching sort of way, making it difficult to turn one's eyes away, as though drawn by an invisible magnet. The momentary meeting of eyes across the room had evoked a stirring within him reminiscent of the feeling he had experienced many years before, when Pauline first came to work at Impact Publicity and for the first time made him want to reach out and touch a woman. It was a sensation he enjoyed, leaving him wishing she would look up again.

At a guess he would have said she was in her mid-twenties, not quite as tall as Pauline, dressed in a black two piece that looked not only smart, but expensive. The black pencil skirt split at the side high enough to attract attention without becoming indecent, hugged the contours of her lower body as it tapered to a point just below the knee. Underneath the black, buttonless jacket she wore a white open-necked blouse. Her blonde hair dropped into curls that danced around her shoulders, but nothing matched the impact of those large, appealing eyes that Greenfield would have defied any man to turn away from.

Seemingly unsettled by his analytical stare, she moved away into the refreshment area, making him feel somewhat embarrassed in the way he used to be. What was it about this woman that she was able to evoke feelings from his past so easily?

Because he was never totally at ease flying, Greenfield disliked the hour or so between check-in and departure, the waiting around serving only to allow time for his apprehension to grow. He tried to convince himself that was the reason for drifting into the refreshment area, not wishing to admit to the alternative attraction. With a cup of coffee he didn't really want, he sat alone at a table, casting his eyes disinterestedly across the front page of the morning paper he had bought earlier on entering the airport. There was a picture of Prime Minister Margaret Thatcher and a lead story reporting Opposition claims that she and the Government were in denial about the country slipping towards recession. Greenfield found politics tiresome, but he did share the concerns around recession. He was picking up some worrying indicators in his business dealings and wondered what recession would mean for his company. Folding the newspaper up and lifting his eyes, he tried to look around without appearing too obvious. The woman who had stirred his senses so was nowhere to be seen.

He was taken aback at the wave of disappointment that swept over him. This was madness. What would he have done if she had been in the room? When had he ever been able to strike up a conversation with a complete stranger, even a male, but especially a female? In the course of his work it was different. There had to be a reason for every meeting, whether with prospective clients or existing ones, so there was always something to talk about to break the ice and maintain conversation. Outside work, he still, as ever, found it virtually impossible. Smiling, he told himself what a fool he was being and picked up his spoon to stir his coffee.

Before he could do so, someone lurched into the side of the table, sending coffee splashing over the rim of the cup. Only an instant reflex action, jumping quickly along the bench seat, enabled him to avoid the hot, spilling liquid. He looked up at the culprit, but any words of admonishment died on his lips at sight of the concern in those big, blue eyes that he thought were lost for ever.

"Oh God, I am sorry," the woman said frantically, sliding into the seat opposite him without waiting for an invitation. "I wasn't looking where I was going."

"It's all right," Greenfield reassured her, "please don't worry about it."

"I have some tissues somewhere." She rummaged desperately in her handbag. "Where the hell are they?"

"Please, it's all right, honestly," he insisted. "I was able to move in time. None of the coffee went on me."

This she was obviously relieved to hear, though the general state of agitation persisted. There was more than a spilt cup of coffee on her mind, he reckoned. She raised her eyes to look at him, but the smile appeared forced. Nevertheless, the same tingle of excitement he had felt a few minutes earlier, when their eyes had met fleetingly for the first time, stirred within him again, only stronger. A female voice on the public address system announced his flight to Barcelona.

"He's not bloody coming, I know it!" She seemed to be talking to herself, as if she had forgotten Greenfield was there. "And he promised this time. He bloody well promised."

For a moment she seemed close to tears. Greenfield leaned towards her, picking up the faintest sensual hint of her perfume.

"Are you all right?" he asked. "Were you expecting someone?"

With a deep sigh, she leaned back in her seat. The tears had not come. Her state of agitation appeared to have been overtaken by one of resignation.

"My husband," she answered quietly. "I am married to what is commonly called a 'workaholic.' He has his own engineering company and seems only to be happy when he's working. He's there all hours of the day or night. Anything or anyone else, including me, comes a very poor second." She gathered up her bag as if to leave. "I'm sorry, I shouldn't be burdening a complete stranger with my troubles."

"My name's Howard Greenfield," he said without the slightest trace of hesitation. "Now we're not strangers anymore, are we?"

He couldn't believe he had really said it. No need to think about it, no building up of courage, it had come straight out. Where was the shyness and awkwardness with members of the opposite sex that had been such a burden to him all his life? What magic spell did this woman weave that could bring out in him such a display of instant confidence?

For several seconds she sat and looked at him, as though deliberating whether to go or stay, uncertain of his directness. He wished he knew what was going through her mind.

"Julie Hutchinson." This time it was a warmer, natural smile. "Where are you off to, Howard?"

"Barcelona."

"For long?"

"Two days, three possibly. Depends how things go."

"Business?"

Greenfield nodded. "I'm afraid so. What about you?"

"I was supposed to be going to Barcelona, too."

"Was?"

"That's the way it looks," she said sadly. "We – my husband and I – have an apartment on the outskirts of Barcelona. I fell in love with the city some years ago when I accompanied my husband on a whirlwind tour of Europe, looking for export orders. It's a big, sprawling monster, always bustling with activity. I feel alive out there, really alive."

"You make it sound very special."

"It is to me. I guess I'm just a big city girl. Trouble is we've hardly ever been back there. Four times this year I've sat here listening to the flight calls. Each time was like today. He never came."

"It can't be easy building up your own business." Greenfield felt obliged to say something in her husband's defence, though reluctant to make too many excuses for him. "New problems must be cropping up all the while. It must be something pretty important to stop him coming."

"The business is built up. He has more than fifty people working for him." She lowered her eyes, staring absently at the table. "The real truth, Howard, is that he just doesn't want to leave it. The place would run itself; he doesn't need to be there. But that's where he wants to be, playing with his lathes, his millers and God knows what other machines, rather than alone with me for a few days."

"Then he's a fool."

Once again Greenfield was stunned by his lack of hesitation. He seemed to be taking on a new personality, becoming a new man. This woman was bringing out in him a measure of assertiveness he would never have thought possible.

Obviously pleased at the flattering response, she managed another smile. "Each time I've gone back home," she went on, "the obedient housewife, making the dutiful sacrifices for a husband who is happier with his machines." The change of mood came suddenly, her tone becoming angry and bitter. "Well sod him, bloody well sod him. This time I am not going home. He can stop on his own and play with his machines. I'm going to have some fun of my own."

The Barcelona flight was called again. Her eyes locked onto Greenfield's, sending a tingle racing through his body, from head to toe.

"Howard, the seat next to me will be vacant," she said. "I would be pleased if you would join me."

Greenfield always found aeroplanes to be claustrophobic, making him feel as though he was sealed up in a closed hollow tube, and normally a cramped, narrow-aisled Boeing 737 did little to relieve this effect. This time, sitting beside Julie, he hardly noticed it. His attention wrapped up entirely in her presence, even the heady feeling that went with the take-off, which usually he found unpleasant, was ignored. Happily, as the aircraft soared upwards towards the sun, he watched her pain drain away, replaced by an aura of contentment, relaxed, but obvious.

Mid-way through the flight, shortly after they had picked tentatively at the functional, but hardly appetising, aeroplane meal, she slipped off her jacket, dropping it lazily against the back of the seat. He swallowed dryly at the sight of her breasts stretching the fabric of the perfectly-tailored white blouse. In crossing her legs the hem of her skirt had travelled up above her knee. Attracting his gaze to her slender legs, it was impossible to ignore the feelings she aroused within him. He told himself repeatedly he was a happily married man with a teenage daughter, a respectable career, a comfortable home and a contented life-style, but it was a lost argument. This young, beautiful woman gave him her full attention, interested in every word he spoke, gently, and affectionately he thought, touching his arm when she laughed or made a special point, and sometimes leaning closer towards him, fleetingly her shoulder brushing his, as she spoke very quietly, as though the words were meant just for him to hear, the rest of the world excluded. As the flight progressed she became increasingly responsive to his presence, allowing him to brush away some straying strands of hair off her forehead and, as he sensed an invitation to become bolder, to playfully squeeze her hand a couple of times. As the conversation turned just a little flirtatious, the full reality of the situation finally hit him. This was not a dream or a daytime sensual flight of imagination; this was really happening and that was the moment he became aware of the feeling that he wanted this woman more than anything in the world.

Knowing it was wrong to feel this urge did not make it go away. He knew he should get up now, move to his own seat, read his newspaper or a book, do anything but remain sitting within the magic reach of the woman who, in a couple of hours, had turned his emotions upside down. But his rekindled ego demanded he stayed where he was.

Yet he was already beginning to have doubts as to whether he could turn the relationship into something more than travelling companions. Though his shyness and awkwardness were gone, his lack of experience remained a handicap. Pauline was the only girl he had ever dated or attempted to date. He was unpractised in judging the mood of a female, guessing how receptive she would be if he asked her out, knowing whether he was underplaying or overplaying his hand. Would Julie agree to a date or would he just be making a fool of himself?

With Pauline it had been different. Seeing her every day in the office had made for a long getting-to-know-you process and allowed plenty of room for procrastination. Then time had been on his side. Now it was his enemy. As the 'plane began its descent into Barcelona airport, he knew that, very shortly, in the warm afternoon Spanish sunshine, Julie could walk out of his life for ever.

Arriving a couple of minutes behind schedule, together with the other passengers they clambered aboard the vehicle ferry that took them from then aircraft to the terminal. Unable to sense what she was thinking or how she felt, he saw his chance rapidly fading away. If only she would give him a sign, just the tiniest of signs.

Finally, she did, more positive than he could ever have hoped for. As they waited in the queue, shuffling slowly through passport control, Julie turned to him and asked, "Howard, is this your first ever visit to Barcelona?

"Actually, yes," he smiled.

"It is such a beautiful city," she said with overwhelming enthusiasm. "You should cancel all your appointments tomorrow and let me show you the sights."

That was the encouragement he needed. True she was only suggesting a sightseeing tour, but the newly-found confidence she had brought out in him pushed him into seizing the initiative.

"There's tonight first," he said boldly. "Have dinner with me."

Her answer came without hesitation. "I would really like that. I know a super little restaurant, serves the best food in Barcelona."

It was done. The deal was struck. He knew then that tonight she would be his and somehow he sensed she knew it too.

"Where are you stopping?" she asked.

"Husa Presidente."

"I know it." As the official rubber stamp thumped down on her passport, she added, "I'll pick you up with a taxi about eight."

Chapter Three

Greenfield began to think she wasn't coming. He looked at his watch again as he shuffled uneasily around the foyer of the Hotel Husa Presidente. It was almost eight-thirty. He should have known it would be like this. Since leaving him at the airport that afternoon, she had been completely in his thoughts. And now she wasn't coming.

His disappointment was close to becoming anguish when she hurried in through the door, sweeping away his desolation as swiftly as she took away his breath. If beautiful was the word to describe her earlier in the day, there were no words superlative enough to do justice to the vision of perfection that stood stunningly before him now, magnificently wrapped in a long, black dress with a wickedly plunging neckline.

"I'm sorry I'm late. Howard," she laughed. "Woman's privilege though, you know."

"I was beginning to think you weren't coming," said Greenfield.

"There was no chance of that." She linked her arm in his. "I've been looking forward to it too much not to come. The taxi is waiting outside for us. I do hope you like Spanish food."

In truth, he didn't, but he would have eaten anything to be with her. It was a happy evening, the soft lights of the restaurant, the romantic sound of the Spanish guitars that accompanied the meal and the heady local wine creating a uniquely relaxing atmosphere of warmth and contentment.

"We'll get a taxi together. He can drop you at your place first," suggested Greenfield, though he had no real intentions of going any further than her apartment.

Yellow taxi cabs buzz around Barcelona like bees around a honey pot, so it was no more than a couple of minutes before they were able to flag one down.

When they arrived at her apartment, only a short drive from the restaurant, he got out of the vehicle with her and paid off the driver. Nothing was said. She didn't invite him in, he didn't ask, but she made no protest. There was now an air of inevitability about the conclusion of the evening.

The apartment was large and luxurious, with a lounge that could have come straight out of one of those glossy magazines that delight in showing homes that most people could never hope to own. While Greenfield sank back into the cushions on the sofa, Julie poured two brandies that looked lost in the bottom of the large, bulbous glasses. When she settled beside him, her closeness overwhelmed him. How much he wanted to reach out and touch her, feel the warmth of her body against his hand.

"What are you thinking about?" she asked softly, looking up at him over the top of her brandy glass.

Her knee fleetingly brushed his as she slightly shifted her sitting position. Greenfield was certain it was no accident.

"I can't believe this is really happening. Can it really be me sitting here alone with the most beautiful woman in the world?" he said, looking deep into her big, blue eyes. "I'm sure I shall wake up any moment and find it's all just a wonderful dream."

Julie smiled and said, "That doesn't answer my question, Howard."

"I'm not sure I should tell you what I'm thinking, you may be shocked."

"Try me. I'm not easily shockable."

"Oh, Julie, you damn well know what I'm thinking," he sighed. "I'm thinking of what it would be like to touch you, kiss you, how it would be to hold your naked body in my arms. I want you more than anything else in the whole world."

Greenfield couldn't believe he had really said that. He had never been able to speak so boldly to a woman before, not even to his wife. Yet with Julie there were no barriers. The inhibitions of a lifetime had melted away. Nothing was beyond his reach tonight.

She showed no signs of being shocked, but said, "I have a husband."

"But he's not here, is he?" he answered. "I am and I think you want me as much as I want you."

His ego was rampant now and demanded to be satisfied. For the first time sexually he felt in control. Never with Pauline, however compliant she tried to be, did he feel totally in control. Tonight with Julie, it was different. In the space of only a few hours this incredible woman had induced in Howard Greenfield a metamorphosis more miraculous than that which turns the unattractive caterpillar into the colourful splendour of the butterfly.

Leaving the sofa, she placed her empty glass on the table and disappeared through a door which could only lead to the bedroom. He was not going to wait till she re-appeared. Tonight he was master of the game.

The bedroom was spacious, housing a large king size bed and other furniture without restricting space for movement. In the centre of the suite of fitted wardrobes lining the wall was a dressing table, with a large, rectangular mirror set against the wall between the table top and overhead cupboards.

Standing in front of the mirror slipping off her earrings, Julie stopped when she saw his reflection as he entered the room. Turning to face him, she loosened the zip at the back of her dress and slipped the thin straps off her shoulders. The dress dropped agonisingly slowly down her body. At last she stood naked before him.

As he rushed forward, she fell into his arms, pressing her lips hard against his. For the first time he experienced the pleasure and excitement of being undressed by a woman. There was also the strange voyeuristic thrill of watching it happen in the mirror behind her as the light caress of her lips followed her hands working their way down the whole length of his body, until his clothes lay in a heap on the floor beside him.

He could wait no longer. Picking her up in his arms, he carried her to the bed. What had seemed an impossible dream a few hours earlier, thirty thousand feet above the spectacularly snow-capped Pyrenees, was about to become reality in the sultry heat of a Spanish summer night.

Carlos watched with weary disinterest, but Alfredo was unable to conceal his excitement. His breathing became noticeably quicker and louder, audible even over the monotonous hum of the movie camera, as he spluttered, "What wouldn't I give to be him at this moment."

"You wouldn't want to be in his shoes," said Carlos.

"For this part I would," insisted Alfredo, his eyes riveted on the rhythmic movement of the naked couple on the bed.

Carlos shrugged. "You've seen it all before," he said. "I don't know why you still get so excited."

"It would be different for you if it were little boys instead of a beautiful woman," retorted Alfredo angrily. "That is more your style, is it not?"

Carlos lapsed into silence, allowing the purring of the camera and the sound of Alfredo's snatched breathing to seemingly fill every corner of the tiny room. It never ceased to amaze Carlos's meagre intelligence that any amount of noise they made could not be heard in the bedroom, just the other side of the wall. The intricacies of sound-proofing and a mirror that allowed him, together with the camera, to look into the bedroom, while providing only the normal reflection on the other side, stretched the limits of his comprehension. It was uncanny to look straight into the eyes of a man and a woman who could see only themselves.

The work Carlos found increasingly distasteful, but it was regular, well-paid and one had to make a living.

"It's over," gasped Alfredo. "My God, how he must feel now."

"It's nothing to how he will feel," said Carlos wearily. "Let's wrap it up and go home."

Chapter Four

The next morning broke hot and sunny, a clear, blue sky blanketing the big city as its wide avenues, lined with palm trees, burst into noisy life. Despite being back in his hotel room only a couple of hours, Greenfield had been unable to sleep, his body riding a peak of exhilaration, inspired by the night's events, that kept him fresh and alive.

Not usually a lover of the Continental breakfast, he was happy today to settle for nothing more than a bread roll and a slice of cheese, so that he could get back quickly to his room to get ready for Julie. His appointments for the day already cancelled, he bathed and shaved, happy in the memories of the previous evening. Time and time again he relived in his mind the moment when he picked her up in his arms, stopping to concentrate on it to the total exclusion of all else, the sensational realisation of a long-standing fantasy.

Physically he was certainly not the strongest of men, so that his wife's persistence in laughing and making herself a dead weight whenever he tried to pick her up in his arms had always made it impossible. With Julie it had been so different. Eager to meet his every demand, satisfy his every whim, she had curled her arms about his neck, taking enough of her own weight to make it possible to lift her effortlessly. What a moment that was!

Normally a tour of the principal sights of a foreign city would be much to his taste, but he had to admit to himself that the only place he really wanted to be was Julie's apartment.

Even though she was extremely punctual this time, he was already waiting outside the hotel when the yellow and black taxi pulled up. She opened the rear door and invited him to join her. Dressed simply in a lemon-coloured, open-necked blouse and black skirt, she still presented a vision so stunning he could only stand and stare in wonder, needing a repeated invitation before climbing in beside her. Greenfield was sure she was the most beautiful woman he had ever seen.

"Where are we off to first?" he asked after a quick welcoming kiss he wished had lasted longer.

"The cathedral," she smiled. "Everyone who comes to Barcelona should see the cathedral."

"Couldn't we just go back to you apartment?"

Julie laughed. "Howard, you are naughty." She linked her arm affectionately in his. "The sights first, my darling. We have the whole day ahead of us."

Greenfield tried hard to appreciate the grandeur of Barcelona Cathedral, built mainly between the end of the thirteenth and middle of the fifteenth centuries, but it was difficult to concentrate his mind on anything but Julie. Her closeness was intoxicating. She led him up the cathedral steps, following in the footsteps of the triumphant Christopher Columbus centuries before, returning from his voyage of discovery to the Americas, into the dark interior, exploring the vast array of candle-lit chapels dedicated to a host of saints he had never heard of. But he could pay only lip-service to her obvious enthusiasm. The only place in Barcelona he really wanted to be was her apartment.

Leaving the cathedral, they wandered leisurely down busy, narrow, shop-lined side streets, Julie pointing out the fairy-tale towers of the Roman Catholic basilica of La Sagradia Familia, the building of which started in 1882, but was still not finished, that dominated the skyline of the Catalan capital city, before picking up another taxi, which swept them past the waterfront monument to Columbus and up a rise overlooking the city.

Even in his preoccupied state, passing through the archway into the Pueblo Español had a measurable impact on Greenfield. It was a visual delight, a Spanish village created by reproducing streets, churches, mansions and dwelling houses, from the different regions of Spain, illustrating the great diversity of the country's architecture.

Arm-in-arm, Greenfield and Julie strolled over cobbled courtyards, past the orange trees, towards the old church, working their way back along the terraces in front of the houses to the bar close to the entrance.

She settled at a table while Greenfield fetched her a glass of white wine and a glass of lager for himself.

After a quick sip of her drink, she said with a hint of sarcasm, "I had better send a postcard to my loving husband in case he hasn't noticed I have gone. I saw some by the entrance when we came in."

"I hope you're not going to say 'wish you were here.' "

She squeezed his arm resting on the table. "Not a chance. I'm very happy with the way things are."

He watched her walk away from him until she had disappeared from sight at the entrance. There was no way he could know he would never see her again.

A tinge of anxiety infiltrated the happiness that had filled his day as the minutes ticked by without her return. It was just at the moment he decided to go in search of her that the shadow fell across him. He experienced an instant tingle of apprehension, a sudden chill deep inside. There was no reason why he should have felt threatened by the outline blotting out the sun, casting its dark reflection over him, yet he was overcome by an unnerving sense of hostility. Suddenly he was filled with a great sense of foreboding.

Swivelling around, Greenfield looked up at two men, both smartly dressed in dark suits and ties despite the midday heat.

"You must come with us now."

It was the slightly taller, slightly younger of the two, who spoke in good, clear English, with only the slightest trace of a European accent. There was no sign anywhere of Julie.

"I'm sorry, I'm not sure I heard you right," replied Greenfield, though he was sure he had.

"I said you are to come with us now."

Greenfield rose hesitantly from the chair. "That's out of the question. I really think you must have mistaken me for someone else. That must be it, a case of mistaken identity."

"There is no mistake."

"I don't know who you are. Are you the police? Have I done something wrong? I really must insist on some sort of explanation or identification, otherwise your request is an impossible one. I don't know you or see any reason why I should go anywhere with you."

The man reached inside his jacket and in the next instant Greenfield found the muzzle of an automatic pistol pressing against his ribcage. Greenfield felt the bubbles of sweat break out on his brow as the man said, "I think this is reason enough."

Greenfield was unable to conceal the look of sheer terror at the sight of the gun pushing against his body. This was madness. What had happened to his idyllic dream? Only minutes before the beautiful Julie, the oh-so-beautiful Julie, had been holding on to his arm, pressing her achingly desirable body against him as they walked. Julie. Jesus Christ, what about Julie?

"The young lady I was with," he spluttered, "what have you done with her? You haven't harmed her?"

"Of course not," replied the man with the gun. "She is a valuable member of the firm, but her job is done now."

The words made no sense to Greenfield. A member of what firm? What was this job she had done? Who were these people who now held him at gunpoint?

The man with the gun grew impatient. "Please do not make a scene, Mr. Greenfield. It is in your best interests to walk quietly to the car waiting for us beyond the entrance. Act normally, as though you are leaving with friends."

Greenfield knew he had little choice, leaving the bar area without further protest, unable to argue with the gun pressed into his back. The second man, who had said nothing, stayed close in an attempt to conceal the pistol from view as much as possible. It was inconceivable that nobody sitting at the other tables had seen the weapon, but, if they had, they chose to ignore it.

As he walked shakily across the cobblestones towards the entrance, the two men kept so close behind him they trod more than once on his heels. Greenfield struggled to find some reason in what was happening. The fact that his name had been used ruled out any lingering possibility of mistaken identity or that this was a random encounter. There had obviously been some measure of pre-planning. But to what end? It had all the appearances of a kidnapping, yet if they knew his name they must know enough about him to be aware he could not raise a large ransom. Whilst being comfortably off, he could hardly be described as a rich man, certainly nowhere near wealthy enough to make all the effort going into this worthwhile.

And what of Julie? He could no longer blind himself to her involvement. Now he knew the truth of what the past twenty-four hours or so had been about. There could be no doubt she had set him up.

As they reached the car, a large dark blue saloon with blacked out windows, the man with the gun partly opened the rear door. A driver was already in position, drumming his fingers impatiently on the top of the steering wheel.

The original nine-stone weakling, Howard Greenfield had always considered himself a physical coward. Even as a boy in school, he had been too frightened to stand up for himself against playground bullies. His shying away from the more adventurous of his contemporaries' playtime pursuits led to him being shunned, so becoming something of a loner. Over the years he had never ceased to marvel at the bravery of ordinary people plunged by circumstances into dangerous situations, sure that in a similar predicament his reaction would be the exact opposite. Until now it had never been put to the test.

Yet fear can be the strangest of motivators. The dividing line between fear and courage is so thin as to become often indistinguishable. So it was with Greenfield. There was a sudden ominous feeling of finality about getting into the car, a cutting off of all hope that provoked an instinctive reaction he would have been incapable of planning in advance.

Putting his hand on the partly open car door, as if to get in, he swung it open with all the force he could muster, hitting the gunman full in the crotch with the wide, shaped outside edge. Taken completely by surprise, the man screamed out as intense pain shot up his body, bringing him helplessly to his knees.

Greenfield ran, driving his legs forward with every ounce of strength and energy he could wring from his out-of-condition body. With no knowledge of the area, he could concentrate only on heading in a downhill direction towards the city. A swift backward glance after twenty paces or so told him the pursuit had only just begun, the silent man and the car driver taking up the chase. Vital seconds had been gained by the unexpectedness of his action, together with their indecision over whether Greenfield or their fallen comrade was the greater priority. The injured man was still down on his haunches, rocking to and fro, gasping with pain. His gun lay on the ground beside him.

While realising the pursuers would be similarly armed, Greenfield reckoned that whatever their purpose, he would not fulfil it as a corpse. The gamble paid off. No shots were fired. Perhaps they did not feel the need, for they were younger as well as fitter, so were gaining rapidly.

Greenfield knew he had to get off the road. His suddenly overworked heart seemed about to explode, pounding against the ribcage as though trying to break through. Desperate gulps of air failed to provide his lungs with an adequate supply of oxygen, so that his breathing became heavy and extremely laboured. There was no way he could outrun these two men in a straight race.

His only chance was in the bushes and trees carpeting the fields that fell down-hill away from the road.

The fence was too high for him to scale in one movement. He tried and failed, banging his legs painfully, as the two men came closer and closer. Sweat ran down his face like water, dropping freely from the tip of his nose and chin. With one almighty, supreme effort, spawned more by sheer determination than anything else, he heaved himself up into a sitting position on top of the wall before swinging his legs to throw himself over to the other side. He never hit the ground he was expecting. Instead, he carried on falling, buffeted by thick-stemmed bushes, angry thorns snatching at his clothes and flesh. The fall seemed endless, an uncontrollable plunge into a bottomless pit. In truth, it was only seconds before he came to rest some twenty feet below the level of the road side of the fence.

There was an overwhelming urge to stay where he was, lying on his back, his eyes closed, resting his aching legs, easing the frightening pounding of his heart. The temptation had to be forced from his mind, as he summoned the will-power to drag himself to his feet. There was no choice. He had to go on.

No broken bones seemed to have resulted from the tumble, the bushes that had bruised and scratched him on the way down also serving to break the fall. But scarcely had he hauled himself to his feet when the two men behind him, younger and more agile, scaled the wall in one movement, only to meet the same unexpected fate. Greenfield once more set off at a run as they hurtled downwards, trying desperately but unsuccessfully to grab hold of the bushes that abused them, until crashing to the ground in a tangled heap. Mercifully, he had regained vital seconds he thought he had lost.

The trees were a last hope. Amongst the trees it was cooler and darker, the large, leaf-filled branches filtering the piercing rays of the sun. Greenfield de-cided to carry out a zigzag manoeuvre, hoping to cause his pursuers some mo-ments of indecision as to his movements, so gaining valuable seconds.

The ploy met with some success, but it was impossible to shake off the men completely and it was rapidly becoming a question of how much longer he could keep going. His rubbery legs, now devoid of any sense or feeling, seemed strangely remote, as though not really part of his body at all. Only the natural will to survive carried him forward.

Suddenly the trees ended and he found himself on a path. Without the wood-land cover it was over. There was no running left in him. Hands on knees, head bent forward gasping for breath, he resigned himself to there being no escape from the two men chasing him. What more could he have done?

The noise hit him all of a sudden. It must have been there since he cleared the trees, but failed to register with his mentally and physically exhausted body. But it was clear and unmistakable – the persistent drone of traffic.

One final effort was needed, one final demand on a body that had already given so much more than he had any right to ask. Teeth gritted, he dragged himself along the path as it skirted the trees until it turned to run alongside an embankment. The two men were already on the path behind him as he scrambled desperately up the grassy bank, emerging between the horizontal poles of a tubular fence, in a serious state of disrepair, onto the pavement alongside a road throbbing with the roar of traffic.

Greenfield couldn't believe his luck when he saw the taxi. Rushing forward to flag it down, his weakened, exhausted body lost its balance, so that he stumbled into the road, bringing the yellow and black cab to a sudden halt amid the squealing of brakes. Ignoring the angry gesticulations of the driver, he yanked open the rear door and threw himself onto the back seat, at the same time screaming, "Hotel Husa Presidente. Rápido! Rápido!"

The taxi driver glowered at him, making no attempt to move, looking him up and down with great suspicion. It was really little wonder. What a mess he must have looked, his face flushed and scratched, hardly able to control his breathing, his shirt, torn with some buttons ripped off, sticking to flesh drenched in sweat.

A quick sideways glance revealed the pursuers coming through the fence onto the pavement. It was going to be too late. They were here, only feet away from him.

"Rápido! Rápido!"

The desperate urgency of Greenfield's pleas finally had an effect. With the two men in pursuit reaching out for the rear door, the driver, shrugging his shoulders in despair while muttering incomprehensibly in Spanish, rammed the taxi in gear, before pulling back into the traffic without so much as a glance in the rear-view mirror.

Greenfield rested his head against the back of the seat, taking deep breaths, trying to regain some composure. For the moment he was safe, but it was certain there was no time to lose. If these people, whoever they were, knew his identity and had gone to such lengths to apprehend him, there could be little doubt they knew where he was staying. Thinking about it now, the whole of the past twenty-four hours seemed unreal, like a short segment of his life that strangely didn't belong to him. If only he could detach it and jettison it, to be lost forever. What a fool he had been. What was it about a man's ego that allowed a beautiful woman to blind him to reality? Julie was so lovely, stunningly so. In truth, there was no way he could have created such an impression on her that she would have wanted him so desperately to commit adultery within a few hours of first meeting him. He had never had that effect on women in his younger days, so he certainly wasn't going to have it now, with a girl probably not that much more than half his age. Yet it had all seemed so plausible. His awakened ego had made him believe only what he wanted to believe. Until now he had not for a second considered the reality of it all.

Julie had weaved a web and dragged him in so easily, as the mythological sirens had lured hapless sailors on to deadly rocks. But for what reason? Greenfield had no intention of staying around to find out. The city held great danger for him now. He would pack his bags, get out to the airport and catch the first flight out on which he could secure a seat, no matter what its destination. Anywhere in the world, it didn't matter. His only interest was to get out of Barcelona.

The journey back to the hotel took less than a quarter of an hour, though it seemed longer. Jumping out of the taxi, Greenfield threw some notes at the driver worth far more than the fare, not stopping to collect his change, as he hurried inside the building. Ignoring the reception clerk's obvious look of disapproval at his appearance, he collected his room key and stepped quickly into the waiting lift, which took him up to the third floor.

Once inside the room, he slammed the door shut and locked it. Suddenly he was trembling, his whole body shaking from head to foot. Unable to control it, he leaned back against the door, his eyes closed. He saw nothing of the figure that had been lurking behind the door, or the pistol barrel that crashed down on the back of his head. There was only a flash of searing pain, then nothing. He never remembered hitting the floor.

Chapter Five

It started as a distant speck of light. He was rushing upwards, being propelled up from the dark bottom of a deep, narrow well at such incredible speed that the speck of light in an instant became a wide opening, which he burst through with a jolt severe enough to make him cry out. Howard Greenfield had regained consciousness.

To start with his mind was a blank. What was he doing here, lying fully-clothed on a small, single bed in a tiny room so unfamiliar to him? Then, as his brain began to function again, so the memories came back, coming together unevenly in a whirlpool of confusion. There was Julie, so beautiful with her big, blue eyes, who had given him new life, albeit for only a very short time. Even now he could close his eyes and still feel her touch. Yet it was madness, for were not the other visions that swirled about in his head her doing, the gun pressed against his ribs, the desperate, panic-ridden flight, the supposed safety of his hotel room., then nothing; until now.

He wasn't prepared for the wave of pain that careered through his head as he hauled himself up into the sitting position. Hands gripped tightly on the edge of the bed, he sat for several seconds, head hung down, eyes tightly closed, allowing the pain to settle and subside, though it eased only slightly. Putting his hand tentatively to the back of his head, he could feel the lump just behind his ear and the dried blood still matted in his hair. Now he knew why he could remember nothing after slamming shut the door of his hotel room.

What light there was coming into the small room in which he now found himself came from a tiny, upright window in the wall opposite the bed. The effort involved in dragging himself across was hardly worth it as the limited view revealed only an area of lawn and one or two trees. He was obviously high up, possibly in what was once a servant's quarters in a large, old house.

A key rattled noisily in the door lock. Pushing open the door, an elderly man, slightly stooped, with hardly any hair on top in contrast to a straggly, greying beard, shuffled inside.

"Ah, Mr. Greenfield, you are awake," he said in English, barely discernible through the heavy accent. He spoke convivially, like a butler greeting a house guest, which irritated Greenfield. "How are you feeling now?"

"Bloody terrible, as someone who has had their skull battered would expect to feel," Greenfield stormed back. "Now who's going to tell me what I'm doing here? I demand to know what the hell is going on."

"You will know very soon now, I would think," said the old man, retreating with an infuriating smile, locking the door behind him.

Five minutes later the door opened again. This time a friendly smile, however false, would have been welcome. Greenfield felt his stomach knot as the man he had poleaxed at the Pueblo Español walked into the room. There was no mistaking the cold look of anger and hatred in his eye. This was a man who craved vengeance. Behind him was his partner, the man of no words, who had led the chase when Greenfield had fled. This time there was nowhere to run. He was at their mercy.

"Believe me Mr. Greenfield, there is nothing I would like better than to tear you apart limb by limb," said the man whom Greenfield had last seen down on his knees in the road. "Unfortunately, I am forbidden to do so. Now you must come with us."

The two men parted to allow Greenfield to walk apprehensively between them, expecting any moment to feel the savage impact of a clenched fist, but it never came. Pushed and prodded down narrow, wooden steps, Greenfield came out on a landing. It was indeed a house of some grandeur, with thick pile carpets and ornately decorated ceilings. After descending a wide, curved marble staircase, the bemused advertising executive was ushered along another carpeted corridor into a large drawing room. The armchairs and settee looked to be genuine antique and there was a beautiful, old, marble fireplace that was obviously no longer used. His escorts closed the door and stood against it, facing forward as though on guard. Greenfield turned to look at them, his face pleading for an explanation, but they remained tight-lipped, staring blankly at him.

Another man entered the room by a door at the far end. Around forty, Greenfield felt, also immaculately turned out, but his elegantly-tailored grey suit together with matching tie, complemented by the thin-rimmed glasses and scattered streaks of grey in his carefully groomed hair, gave him a look of distinction the others couldn't match.

"Good afternoon, Mr. Greenfield, my name is Richards, John Richards. It's not my real name, of course, but it will suffice for the purpose of this discussion." There was a definite American accent. "I hope your head is not too painful."

The words made Greenfield suddenly aware again of the throbbing, hammering pain, which had faded strangely into the background as his mind had become preoccupied with his renewed encounter with the two gunmen and the descent down the stairs.

"It's as painful as you would expect when your skull has just been split open by a blunt instrument," he retorted angrily.

"Yes, the use of force was regrettable," sympathised Richards, "but it really was your own fault, you know. You had your chance to come without any fuss."

"At gunpoint? A complete stranger pokes a gun in my belly and tells me to go with him and I should just get up and do so without any fuss?"

Richards nodded. "Most usually do. You were a brave man, Mr. Greenfield, and, though you caused us much inconvenience, we have to give you credit for that."

"I wasn't brave, I was scared, scared out of my mind. In the end I was stupid, too. I thought in my hotel room I was safe, for a little while anyway."

Richards allowed himself a smug smile. "We like to cover every possibility. Our professionalism is something we pride ourselves on."

"Professionalism at what?" The calmness in Greenfield's manner and voice was forced only with the greatest of effort. He remained a very frightened man. "Who are you? What do you want with me? If you are looking for some sort of ransom, I could raise only a small one, certainly not large enough to justify the trouble you have gone to."

Richards shook his head. "Your money is of no interest to us, Mr. Greenfield. It is expected you will be much more useful to us than that." There was a pause as Richards leaned against the wide mantelpiece above the big, redundant fireplace. "We are an international organisation offering specialist services to a clientele that demands only the best and is prepared to pay a lot of money to get it. We are recruiting you, Mr Greenfield, to carry out one of these services for us."

"I'm an advertising executive, for Christ's sake!" protested Greenfield. "I can not see what possible service I could be to people who threaten, physically assault and carry guns. Besides, what's to stop me agreeing to anything you say here and now and going straight to the police as soon as you put me back on the street?"

With a heavy sigh, Richards moved back to the door through which he had entered the room. "I am beginning to find your lack of co-operation somewhat tiresome, Mr. Greenfield. Before we go any further with this conversation, there is something I think you should see."

Silently obeying what seemed more like an order than a suggestion, the advertising executive followed Richards into a small, windowless room. The wall to the right was covered by a celluloid screen, in front of which were two chairs. After guiding Greenfield to one, Richards sat in the other. The two heavies closed the door behind them, taking up sentry-like positions.

As the lights dimmed, a brief shaft of light shot from a small square opening in the wall behind them, cutting through the darkness to illuminate the big screen. What was happening now? Had they stopped for a film show? Despite the presumed seriousness of his situation, this was becoming so bizarre to Greenfield he had to struggle to suppress the urge to laugh out loud.

Any such inclination died instantly in his throat as the screen flickered into life. There was no mistaking Julie, those beautiful eyes looking straight out at him, slipping off her earrings. He recognised her surroundings as the bedroom of her apartment and the first fearful inkling of what was happening crept into his brain. He prayed that he was wrong, but it took only seconds for his worst fears to be confirmed as he saw himself enter the bedroom behind the girl. He broke out in a cold, clammy sweat as he watched her dress slide gently down her back, falling into a crumpled heap at her feet.

The film recorded every detail as Julie, in her nakedness, undressed him. His stomach churned, nausea sweeping over him, as he watched her kiss seemingly every inch of his body, working down to his penis, caressing it with seemingly eager lips, taking it into her mouth. All the time his face, showing varying expressions of sexual delight, looked out at him from the screen.

The nausea that gripped his body forced him to retch, but nothing came up, his stomach continuing to turn over inside him.

"No more! I don't want to see any more!" he yelled, bending forward to rest his head on his knees, desperate to put the image that filled the wall before him out of sight.

"Enough," snapped Richards. The film stopped and then disappeared from the screen. The dimmed lights became bright again.

"What kind of people are you?" Greenfield turned to look at Richards, who had stood up and stepped back when the vomit had threatened. Then, for the second time that day, Greenfield was roused by an extreme of emotion into an action totally alien to the weak, cowardly character he saw himself as. This time it was anger, surging through him like a rushing, unstoppable torrent of water bursting through a crumbling, broken dam, sweeping the sickness away before it, filling his insides instead with a rage that grew by the second.

"What kind of people are you?" he said again, but this time it was drawn out, rising in volume until at the finish it was a scream as he hurled himself forward from his chair. This was something Richards wasn't expecting. Caught by surprise, the impact of Greenfield's onrushing body sent him reeling back against the wall. Fired by the anger that consumed him, Greenfield had momentarily lost all control. If he had retained any degree of rationality during those few seconds, he would have realised the futility of his action. Richards had become the focal point for his rage to the exclusion of all else. The other two men in the room were forgotten. But this lapse of memory lasted no longer than the very short time it took them to cross the room and bring the full weight of their bodies down upon him. On crashing to the floor beneath them, a searing pain shot through his head from the wound at the back of his skull inflicted earlier in his hotel room. He felt as though his head would explode as the world seemed to spin away from him. Satisfied that he was a spent force, the two men lifted themselves off him before hauling him to his feet by his arms. When they withdrew their support, his legs buckled and only their swift grab for his arms prevented him from hitting the floor again.

"I'm glad you finally appreciate the gravity of your situation," said Richards, straightening his expensive suit, "but I wish you had chosen a less aggressive way of showing it."

The words drifted as if from a great distance into Greenfield's world of semi-consciousness, but they were no less comprehensible. The gravity of his situation was now beyond dispute. But what was his situation? What was really happening to him? He was just a man who sold advertising on a business trip. What had he got to offer these people?

Richards' words drifted through again.

"You will be taken to a bathroom down the hallway to recover and clean yourself up. Then we will resume the chat we were having before you saw our little film."

The pain in Greenfield's head had subsided into a dull throb. He had stopped the bleeding from a cut sustained on his lip sometime during the melee in the projection room and even managed to remove some of the dried blood matted in his hair around the wound opened by the pistol-whipping, but there was little to be done about the bruising beginning to materialise on his cheekbone. The two men were waiting outside for him. There was no point in delaying the moment any longer. Whatever was going to happen to him was going to happen. Time was irrelevant.

He leaned forward towards the mirror running along the wall of the bathroom, his arms outstretched, resting on the edge of the sink. Looking at the bruised, forlorn face that stared sadly back at him, he muttered, "Oh, Julie, what have you done to me?"

Chapter Six

Greenfield was led back to the large drawing room. Richards was waiting, having changed his suit, though the advertising man was sure he had done no permanent damage to the other one when he had charged at Richards in the projection room. Perhaps crumpled it a little, but obviously enough to offend this man's pride in his immaculate appearance. This time the suit was a dark blue pin-stripe, looking equally expensive, with, of course, a tie matched perfectly. Here was a man who undoubtedly liked the finer things, but Greenfield was decidedly dubious about the origins of the wealth that enabled him to afford them. His misgivings were about to be confirmed.

"Please sit down, Mr. Greenfield," requested Richards, gesturing to a large armchair. Greenfield moved forward, leaving the other two men at their station by the door. "I trust you are now going to exercise some control over your emotions and we are not going to see a repetition of the unfortunate scene a little while back. Please believe us, we have no wish to hurt you any more than we have to."

Greenfield said nothing. Though unimpressed by the apparent concern for his welfare, he knew he could do little else but listen to what this man had to say.

"Having seen the film," Richards went on, "you hardly need me to point out that you have little choice but to agree to our demands. However, as I said before, we are not interested in your money. We simply want you to join us. You will become one of our operatives."

"Operatives?"

"Yes, you will carry out an assignment for us."

"Let me remind you I am a business executive. I know nothing of your world. I don't see how I can possibly do anything for you."

"On the contrary, your position in life makes you ideal for what we have in mind," insisted Richards. "A highly respected member of the community, above suspicion. And you have a great deal to lose should you fail to carry out your allotted task."

A shiver ran up Greenfield's spine. He did have a lot to lose.

"Just what is it you expect me to do?"

Richards, who had remained standing, looked up at the ceiling, as if for inspiration, then straight at Greenfield.

"We – that is the organisation, of course – carry out a number of specialised services, but these consist mainly of the gathering of information that may be of interest to our clients and elimination on request."

"Elimination on request?"

"Yes, Mr. Greenfield and that is where you are going to help us."

Greenfield's eyes widened, his mouth dropped open. He made no sound, Richard's words stunning his brain so that any immediate response was impossible.

"This is crazy," he spluttered finally. "You make it sound as though you're expecting me to kill someone."

"Such an ugly word, Mr. Greenfield. Don't you think 'eliminate' has a softer, more professional ring to it?"

"You're all mad," Greenfield protested loudly. "I demand you end this nonsense now."

"I'm afraid you are the only one here talking nonsense, Mr. Greenfield, and I can't believe you do not realise now you are in no position to demand anything. Please remember our little film."

"But I work in advertising," protested Greenfield. "I'm no hit man."

Richards smiled. "Such a quaint expression, but one rarely used in our circles. We prefer to call our people 'operatives.'"

"It's a joke." Greenfield threw up his arms in a gesture of despair. "It's elaborate and it's sick – my God it's sick – but it has to be somebody's idea of a joke."

Richards sighed. "When will the English realise that their inclination to see a joke in every situation can be rather tiresome to other nationalities." There was no sign of humour in his face as he added, "I think this is no laughing matter for you, Mr. Greenfield."

Greenfield sank back into the chair. "How do you know I'm capable of killing someone?"

"Wouldn't you have killed me a short while ago if you hadn't been stopped?"

"To be honest, I don't know. But that was different anyway. That was in the heat of the moment, fired by anger, humiliation and hate, even, all directed at you. Killing somebody in cold blood with premeditation is a different proposition. What make you think I can do that?"

"It's not so different as you might think." Richards sat down on the large settee, his hand brushing an imaginary speck of dust from his immaculately creased trousers. "None of us really knows what we are capable of. We find out as we go along, as circumstances dictate. You, more than anybody, must be aware of that today." Richards leaned forward towards Greenfield. "You will do what we ask because you have to; it's as simple as that. Should you fail to carry out your assigned task, the film you have seen this afternoon will be processed onto a number of video tapes and circulated to anyone we feel should see it. Your wife will see it, as will your daughter; your employers will receive a copy and we will ensure it is well-circulated within your daughter's school. Can you imagine how your daughter will feel seeing her father on that film? Can you imagine the humiliation of her facing her friends at school after they have seen the film? And what of your wife? Will she welcome you with open arms after seeing your on-screen performance? I think not. Your life, as you know it, would be over. The career you have worked so hard and long to build up would lie in tatters at your feet. Your wife and daughter would despise you. No, Mr. Greenfield, when the time comes, my bet is that you will find it easier to pull the trigger."

"How do you know about my wife and daughter?" demanded Greenfield with some urgency. "What have you done to them?"

"Not a thing," assured Richards calmly. "Your wife and daughter are in no direct physical danger from us. We know about them because we do our job very thoroughly. Most people who travel with some regularity come under our scrutiny to judge their potential as operatives. Suitable candidates are selected very carefully. Obviously, they must have a lot to lose, but, more importantly, care about losing it. We felt you fitted the bill better than most."

"And just who am I expected to kill?"

Greenfield couldn't believe the words that came out of his mouth. Had he really asked that question?

"I have no idea at this moment in time. It could be months before you are allocated a target. You will be informed and provided with a weapon, almost certainly a gun in your case."

"But I've never fired a gun in my life," protested Greenfield. "I've never even handled one. We are led to believe there really are people who make a living doing this sort of thing. Surely you would be better off with one of them."

Richards shook his head. "Hit men, as you like to call them and their methods of operating become known to Interpol and police forces over a period of time. Used regularly, there is always the possibility of one eventually getting caught and traced back to us. You will be used only once. That greatly reduces the odds of such a catastrophe. And, of course, such people cost a lot of money. We have to be cost effective.

"It's because you are not a professional assassin that your accuracy with a gun is not important. Who would ever suspect you? You are a respected member of the community. You will never have had any personal contact with your selected target. You have no record of violence, no criminal record, not even a parking ticket. No known contacts with crime, organised or otherwise. All you have to do is use your common sense. Choose your moment with care and dispose of the weapon sensibly, although it is not a major problem if it is found. Our guns are hand-made within the organisation. We prefer they are not found, but, should they be, it would be impossible to trace their origin.

"The person you kill will not know you or have any reason to suspect you. This is why accuracy is not important. You will be able to get so close that missing will be impossible. It will simply be a case of pointing the gun and pulling the trigger. Then you run." After a brief pause, Richards added, "What you, Mr. Greenfield, would call a hit-and-run man."

He laughed loudly.

Greenfield stared incredulously at this man who could take him so clinically through the pros and cons of committing murder yet, in the same breath almost, laugh so heartily at what he obviously considered to be a worthy example of his own wit.

Seeing that Greenfield was not sharing his amusement, Richards curtailed his laughter. "I'm sorry, Mr. Greenfield, I was under the impression you liked a little joke. The English tradition to make jokes in adversity."

"I see nothing amusing in my situation, Mr. Richards."

All traces of humour disappeared from Richard's face. "I'm glad you finally understand your position," the man said solemnly. "Providing you ensure no-one actually sees you pull the trigger, there will be absolutely nothing to connect you with the killing. None of our operatives have ever been caught. You are an intelligent man, Mr. Greenfield, so we do not expect you to be the first."

"What if I were?"

"I think that would be your problem more than ours. Without hard evidence to back it up, do you think anyone would believe your story?"

"So what happens now?"

"You will go about your business in Spain as though nothing has happened. Then you will return home and carry on your life as normal. You will be informed when we require your services. It could be days, weeks, months even. I think that concludes our business for today, Mr. Greenfield. Now you will be brought some refreshment and returned to your hotel."

Richards rose carefully, smoothing his suit with his hands.

"Please do not consider going to the police," he went on. "It's highly unlikely you would be able to find your way back here with them or, I would think, to the apartment where you put on such an admirable performance for us. Was that not a night to remember, Mr. Greenfield? Anyhow, the journey there was in the dark; you were not taken by a direct route and you most certainly had your mind on other things. And, of course, copies of the film will have been seen by relevant people before you reach home. You are dealing with powerful forces here, Mr. Greenfield. Believe me, we do not make idle threats."

Richards crossed to the door, pausing as he exited between the two guards. Turning, he added, "A final thought. Do not think that taking the honourable way out would spare anyone. Should you take your own life, the films will still go out."

"You bastard!"

It was a long, drawn-out yell that vented Greenfield's feelings of anger, fear and revulsion, but appeared to have no effect on Richards, who calmly shut the door behind him as he left the room. There was a noticeable tensing of the other two men, in obvious anticipation of a possible repeat of their captive's earlier attack, but there was no fight left in Greenfield now. These people had him exactly where they wanted him. He had to accept there was nothing more he could do.

The elderly gentleman, who had greeted him earlier in the room upstairs, brought him a tray of food and coffee. If he had eaten anything, he was sure he would have been ill, but, his mouth and throat very dry, Greenfield readily swallowed the hot coffee.

It took only a few minutes for the drug to take effect. When he woke up it was to find himself, with a sore head, lying on the bed in his hotel room.

Chapter Seven

Tommy Morgan hated his one-room bedsit. Undoubtedly, it had been a fine, large bedroom for someone many years before, when the house would have almost certainly have been occupied by a family of fairly substantial means, but as a living room, bedroom and kitchen rolled into one, it served poorly.

Rented as "furnished" accommodation, the furniture consisted of an old two-seater settee and armchair, which Morgan presumed to be a match, though the pattern was so faded and grimy it had passed beyond recognition, a rickety tubular-legged coffee table with grubby, Formica top and a small wardrobe set against the wall. The threadbare carpet covered only half the floor, surrendering the rest to bare floorboards. A single bed was tucked against the wall, adjacent to the wardrobe. A tatty, plywood partition cut off the kitchen, which really was nothing more than an electric cooker, old enough surely to be approaching heirloom status, and a small sink.

Morgan shuddered despite wearing a thick, woollen pullover. The early November chill easily overcame the meagre warmth thrown out by the up-right paraffin heater, his only source of heating. He lived for the day he would get out of this place and that surely couldn't be much longer. There had to be contact soon.

Morgan's apartment was one of two in the upstairs of the house, the other occupied by George, a young man of questionable mental capacity, who had a regular Friday night ritual, whereby he indulged himself throughout the evening in the local pub to such a degree it became a race against time, on his return, to reach the communal lavatory at the far end of the landing before bringing most of it back again, an awful waste of good beer, Morgan always thought. To his credit, George usually made it in time, but the accompanying sound effects that echoed in the old house were something Morgan could have happily lived without.

Life in this hovel did, however, have its lighter moments, provided mainly by George's inclination to sleepwalk around the house naked. There was one memorable night when, wakened by the screams of the elderly spinsters who occupied the only ground floor apartment, Morgan had flown down the stairs expecting to find murder, rape or robbery in progress. Instead he found George, as naked as the day he was born, standing at the open door, while the two women, screaming heartily, cowered within. Morgan had carefully guided him back to his room, but was never sure whether he really was sleepwalking or not. After all, it had been a Friday night!

The electric kettle clicked off. Dropping a tea bag in a mug, Morgan poured in the hot water. As he fetched the milk bottle from the kitchen, there was a knock on the door.

"Who is it?"

"Electricity Board, sir. There seems to be a fault on your meter."

"It's downstairs, by the front door."

"We know where the meter is, sir." There was no attempt to hide the note of impatience in the voice. "We need to check some of the wiring in the flat."

Morgan cursed as he put the milk bottle down on the coffee table and crossed to the door. Why did interruptions always come just when a cup of tea or a meal had been put on the table? He had opened the door barely an inch before it was shoved open with great force, sending him reeling backwards, tipping over the coffee table to crash to the floor amid a scattering of hot tea and splashing milk.

The room was spinning. He knew he had to stabilise, clear away the fog from his eyes. There was a vague image of two men as he was hauled to his feet. The breath was knocked out of him as a fist hammered into his stomach. Another fist followed up, smashing into his face. Blood flowing freely from his nose, his legs buckled and he once more crashed to the floor. As the figure loomed over him again, he lashed out with his feet, just about making contact. His attackers stepped back, but the respite lasted only a moment. They came again, skirting his lashing feet, to haul him up with a heavy thud against the wall. Bleeding, hardly able to see and gasping for breath, he was powerless to resist the fists pounding his body and face.

As if by instinct his mind continued to work while his body succumbed to the onslaught, searching for a way out. He needed a weapon of some sort if he was to have any hope of fighting back. The milk bottle; where was the milk bottle? The succession of blows taking their toll, he slid down the wall, clattering again to the floor. Through the mist clouding his eyes, he could just make out the blurred outline of the bottle lying beside the overturned coffee table, about four feet away. It was his only chance. A desperate lunge through the feet of his assailants and it was in his hand. Summoning all his remaining strength, he brought the bottle down on the edge of the coffee table, smashing the bottle in half. Sitting on the floor, he turned, clutching the milk bottle neck as he pushed the jagged, broken edge towards his attackers. The two men held back, giving Morgan the vital seconds he needed to clear his head.

Everything drifted back into focus as he managed to lift himself shakily to his feet. The blows he had taken to his stomach made him feel sick. Blood pouring from his mouth and nose dripped off the end of his chin. He could actually feel his left eye swelling. But he was ready for them now. The element of surprise was gone and his makeshift weapon levelled the odds somewhat. Brandishing the broken bottle in his right hand, he beckoned the two men forward with his left.

"Come on, then," he challenged. "Let's see how brave you are now."

"I think we've had enough for now, Mr. Morgan."

Another man had entered the room, older than the other two, with hardly a hair on his head, but a thick, bushy beard, as though all his hair was growing in the wrong place.

"Who the hell are you?" demanded Morgan. "Who the hell are any of you?"

"Most people call me 'the Beard' for rather obvious reasons," said the new arrival. "Now do put down the bottle, please."

"Only if you call off Pinky and Perky here."

The two men reacted to the taunt, but as they moved forward Morgan lashed out with the broken bottle, drawing the jagged edge across the wrist of the one nearest to him. There was a startled cry as blood oozed from the severed skin.

"I said that's enough," shouted the Beard.

Morgan was unsure whether it was he who was being admonished or the two muscle men. To the latter the Beard added, in calmer tone, "Leave us. Get that wrist fixed. You're bleeding all over the man's floorboards."

The two men hesitated.

"Go on," insisted the Beard. "I'll be all right."

Seemingly satisfied, they departed through the open door, leaving a trail of blood spots across the floor. Shutting the door behind them, the Beard made a quick survey of the cheerless room that passed for an apartment.

"God, do you really live in this dump?"

"It's all I can afford."

"Or the Social Security can afford."

"That's none of your bloody business."

"Put down the bottle, Mr. Morgan." When he made no move to do so, the Beard added, "You're being very foolish. I am armed."

He opened his unbuttoned overcoat and jacket to reveal the butt of a pistol poking out from under his armpit, secured in a holster clipped to a strap tightened around his shoulder.

Righting the coffee table, Morgan dropped the broken bottle on to the patterned top, awash with a gooey mixture of tea, milk and blood. His nose was still bleeding, though now reduced to a trickle.

"I need a towel or something for my face."

"Okay, but don't do anything silly," agreed the Beard, wondering about the slight, yet unmistakeable, hint of an Irish accent in Tommy Morgan's speech.

In the kitchen Morgan soaked a towel in cold water. Returning to sit on the edge of the bed, resting his painful, battered face in the wet towel, he asked, "Now what's this all about?"

"You've been asking questions, my friend. Too many questions in the wrong places."

"I don't consider us to be friends and it would seem I've been asking them in the right places."

"Don't try to be too smart, Mr. Morgan." The Beard dropped into the well-worn armchair. "Your position is not a very healthy one. The people I represent don't much care for someone poking around asking questions. It draws attention to them and they get a little edgy."

"I had to find a firm big enough to handle the deal we're offering." The towel was now stained red, but the cold water had stemmed the bleeding completely. The eye felt as though it was still swelling.

"Who are we?"

Morgan hesitated. Spotting the electric kettle, dented and upside-down on the floor, he found himself wondering if it would still work. Why couldn't they have waited until he had drunk his cup of tea?

"We are an army at war. We fight to remove the shackles of British oppression that has blighted our country for centuries."

"The I.R.A.?" The Beard raised his eyebrows in surprise.

"I'll say no more. Draw your own conclusions."

"Well, well, well." The Beard stood up to examine the curtains, once a bright yellow, but dulled by years of accumulated dirt. "Christ, don't you ever wash these?"

"I didn't come all the way from Ireland to wash curtains."

"Suppose you tell me what you did come for."

"To make a deal. We need money urgently for weapons and ammunition."

"Yes, you've had a bad time lately, haven't you?" The Beard detached himself from the grimy curtains with a gesture of disgust. "Quite a few of your men killed or caught, your secret weapon hideaways uncovered. Lost a few rifles too many, eh?"

"We're talking much more than a few rifles. We have spectacular plans to intensify the fight against oppression. We can win this war, but it costs a lot of money. I put myself at considerable risk coming over here. I am not exactly unknown to the police and security forces. I am not taking that chance for a few rifles."

"All right, Mr Morgan, just what is it that you are offering for sale?"

"Heroin." Morgan looked for a reaction from the Beard, but there was none. "Top grade stuff, you'll never be offered better."

"Street value?"

"Around four million."

This time there was a reaction in the form of an audible gasp. For a few seconds there was silence as the Beard stared hard at Morgan. Then he said, "Are you telling me you have four million pounds' worth of heroin tucked away?"

"Yes and it's here in the country. Within an hour of agreeing a price it could be in your hands. Cash on delivery, of course."

"How the hell did you get your hands on that?"

"That's my business."

"If you want to deal, mister, you had better make it my business." A note of menace had crept into the Beard's voice that made Morgan feel a little uneasy. "Now where does a bunch of toy soldiers like you lay its dirty, little hands on four million pounds' worth of heroin?"

Now it was Morgan's turn to react. Standing up angrily, he stabbed a threatening finger in the direction of the Beard and cried, "That's enough of the insults. I'll not stand by and let you belittle the brave men who fight for the freedom of my country."

"Oh, and what are you going to do about it then?" taunted the Beard, moving a couple of paces closer to the Irishman. "Do you need to look in a mirror to see what a mess your face is? Believe me, it wouldn't take much arranging for it to be made more of a mess. One of the reasons for this little demonstration here today was to show you the sort of forces you are dealing with, but I have to wonder if the message has got home. If you don't want a repeat performance, I suggest you tell me where this heroin has come from."

Morgan had little choice. The deal had to be made.

"Libya."

The Beard grunted in disbelief. "Gift-wrapped by Colonel Gaddafi, you're going to tell me next."

The Irishman was becoming frustrated. "What the hell's the matter with you? We have a lot of friends out there. Our men train there for active duty. It's Pakistan heroin obtained for us by our friends in Libya. I'm offering your organisation a five-star deal and you treat me like shit."

"You are shit, Mr Morgan," snapped the Beard, "but that doesn't necessarily mean we won't deal with you. What sort of price are you looking for?"

"Three million."

"That's a lot of money."

"And a lot of profit."

"There are certain overheads to be met."

"Bullshit!" Morgan was adamant. "The price is not for haggling. Three million, not a penny less."

After brief consideration, the Beard replied, "It's too big for me to make a decision on, I'll have to report back. This one will have to be decided at the highest level."

"Then that's who I'll deal with," said Morgan. "I want to see your top man."

"Impossible. You'll deal through me."

"Then it's no deal. I want to deal with the man who can make the decision. I should wait and see how impossible he thinks it is after he has heard what's on offer."

"We shall need a few days to consider what you say, Mr Morgan. Do you know the Mole with Two Heads not far from here?" The Irishman nodded. "Be there a week today about eight. We will, of course, require sample of the goods."

"You shall have it," agreed Morgan. "A week today."

The Beard paused at the door. With one last sweeping look at the apartment, he said, "You live in a pigsty, Mr. Morgan. It's disgusting."

Ten minutes later Morgan also left the building and made a short walk to the nearest phone box. When the number he dialled was answered, he said simply, "It looks as though we're on."

It hurt too much to smile.

Chapter Eight

Howard Greenfield tried hard to carry on with life as normal, but it was proving impossible. Although it was nearly eight weeks since Barcelona, he had heard nothing. The whole ghastly episode had now become a great burden to him, which every day's waiting only added to. It was a nightmare from which there seemed no awakening. He had become moody, edgy, speaking little at home, contributing nothing to the family life that now seemed so precious to him.

Many times over the past two months he had reflected on what he saw as one of life's greatest ironies in that you never really appreciate the worth of the things closest to you, the everyday things you take unthinkingly for granted, until you stand on the brink of losing them. The presence of his wife and daughter with the joy and contentment they brought him, the comfort and security of his home, the position he had attained at work, all figured in a new awareness of the importance of facets of his life that had become an accepted part of his daily routine. Now the future of a life he had strived for more than twenty years to achieve swung on whether he could kill in cold blood someone who would be a complete stranger. Failure to do so, when the time came, would see everything wiped out in a mere fraction of the time it had taken to build it up.

Greenfield was in no doubt that these people, whoever they were, would carry out their threat. What filled him with revulsion more than anything was the thought of his daughter seeing the film of him and Julie. Obviously, it would be a great shock to his wife and there was every chance she would never want to lay eyes on him again, yet she was mature enough, in time, to come to terms with it. But what effect would it have on a fourteen-year-old girl? It would probably scar her mentally for the rest of her life.

Even so, Greenfield was not one hundred per cent sure he could actually pull the trigger that would keep the lives of him and those around him intact. To calculatedly wipe out the life of another human being was something he found it difficult even to contemplate. There persisted a strange aura of unreality about his having to think on such a subject, yet the reality of his predicament was inescapable. Would it come easily when the moment came? Or would his finger freeze on the trigger, unable to carry through the act that would be his salvation.

These thoughts had kept his mind in turmoil since returning from Spain. One day he would feel he could kill, hold on to life as he knew it. The next day there would be doubts. He saw himself holding the gun out in front of him in both hands, his brain willing to fire, but his fingers not responding, as though they were no longer part of his body. Which road would he go down when the moment of truth finally arrived? The scales were finally poised. What was going to tip them one way or the other?

Despite his personal problems, the trip to Barcelona had been a huge success from a work point of view. Jason Henderson, his managing director, had showered praise on him. There had even been a memo of congratulations from the chairman of Ibex Holdings, the group of companies to which Impact Publicity Services belonged. At the office, Greenfield was riding the crest of a wave, never being held in higher esteem.

At home it had been so different. The lump on the back of his head was almost gone now, but it had been badly discoloured and open across the top, occasionally seeping blood.

Pauline appeared to have accepted, reluctantly, his explanation that he had slipped on a flight of stone steps at the office of a client. What she failed to understand was his vehement resistance to her pleas for him to see the family doctor. For Greenfield it was too risky. An expert eye may have recognised it as a result of a blow from a pistol barrel or a similar blunt instrument. There would inevitably have been heavy pressure to report it to the police and he was in no position to explain to anybody why that was impossible.

Returning home from work on a wet November evening in the dreary rush hour crawl, he looked around at the nose-to-bumper cars, the crowded double-decker buses, people scurrying along the pavement in the persistent downpour and the occasional lone maverick pedestrian who darted between the stop-start traffic. Somewhere out there was the man or woman he would be expected to kill. What was this person doing right now, at this very moment? What emotions was he or she experiencing? Was life happy or sad? Did this person really deserve to die? What did one have to do to deserve to die?

Where was Julie at this moment, he wondered. This was a woman he had every reason to hate, yet it had proved impossible to completely shake the memory of that night in Barcelona. This shocked Greenfield and he hated himself for it. Even knowing the true reasons for everything she did that night couldn't stop his reliving the feel of her naked body in his arms or the ecstatic feelings she had aroused and so expertly satisfied. There were even nights when he lay in bed wishing it was Julie lying beside him instead of his wife. For all this he could offer no explanation, knowing only that it brought on feelings of great shame and guilt, which added to the heavy burden he already carried.

Pulling his company-owned two-litre Rover onto the drive of his home, he switched off the engine and sat for a few minutes watching the rain fill in the arches cut in the windscreen by the wipers. There was no longer any joy in coming home. Tangled emotions of fear, apprehension, shame and guilt made him uncomfortable with his wife and daughter, subdued, moody and depressed. He lived in dread of the telephone ringing, hardly daring to answer it. The longer the waiting went on, the greater the anguish became. What a mess his life had become. His own sullen moodiness must now surely be threatening the very existence he wanted so desperately to preserve; may have to kill for, even. He began to wonder if his life would ever return to normal.

That evening followed a familiar pattern. The meal was served and eaten without a word being spoken, the only noise being the scraping of cutlery on the plates, made to sound all the louder by the silence. When the meal was over, his daughter left the table, returning upstairs to her bedroom to finish her school homework. Normally Pauline would then begin clearing the table. Tonight, however, she remained sitting, staring at her husband. Locked in his thoughts, Greenfield was unaware of the change in routine until his wife's voice broke through the mental barrier.

"We have to talk, Howard."

"Not now," he replied wearily.

"Yes, now!" she snapped.

Greenfield looked up, startled by the anger in her tone. It wasn't like Pauline to raise her voice in anger. It was there in her eyes too, that looked deep into his. God knows, he sympathised with the stress she must be under, but he was helpless to do anything about it.

"What's happening to us, Howard?" Pauline went on, regaining her composure.

Greenfield sighed. "I know things are difficult at the moment. I've things on my mind, things I have to sort out. It will pass, I promise."

Pauline put her hand on his. "Howard, if you have problems, let's talk about it. Is it work? Is there something here at home? Tell me. Please."

If only it could be so. How dearly he would love to take her in his arms, hold her close to him, tell her everything, unburden his mind, ask her advice about the deadly dilemma he faced. If only…but it was impossible.

"I can't tell you, my love," he said. "It's something I have to work out for myself."

"Surely I can help."

"No, not this time. I'm sorry, you just can't."

Pauline drew her hand away. Her voice trembled, but she held back the tears.

"What really happened in Barcelona?"

The question hit Greenfield like a punch to the stomach. He struggled to gather together his thoughts, keep his composure. She couldn't know anything. Surely that was impossible.

"Why do you ask that?" he queried with a forced air of calmness.

Pauline was not impressed. "Oh, come on, Howard, don't treat me like a fool," she exploded, the tremble in her voice giving way once more to anger. "You come back with a lump on your head the size of a golf ball. You don't talk anymore or take an interest in anything. You just skulk around with an end-of-the world look, moody, unsmiling. Don't tell me nothing happened in Barcelona."

"I explained the lump on my head."

"Oh yes, the fall on the steps. I didn't think much of that explanation at the time, Howard; I think even less of it now."

"Would I lie to you, Pauline?"

Silence fell as she considered her answer. It must only have been a few seconds, yet to Greenfield it seemed never-ending.

"Up to a few weeks ago I would have said 'no'," she answered quietly. "Now I'm not so sure."

"So my own wife calls me a liar."

47

"I say what I feel, Howard."

He had to end this conversation, get out of the house. Without another word he went into the hallway to get his coat. As Pauline heard the door slam behind him, so the barriers that had held back the tears crumbled.

At eleven o' clock she received a telephone call from the manager of the local public house suggesting she might fetch her husband rather than let him drive home in his condition. Not relishing the prospect of an unpleasant cleaning job, Pauline made sure she had a paper bag with her when she got into her brand new Rover Metro. She eased the car out onto the road, trying to remember if she had ever known her husband the worse for drink before. She collected him, as she felt duty-bound to do so. Not a word was exchanged between them on the way home.

Chapter Nine

Tommy Morgan began to think no-one was coming. An hour and a couple of pints since his arrival at the Mole With Two Heads, he still sat alone, beginning to wonder if he had got the right pub or the right day even. There was still some pain from the bruises and swelling on his face, but if he could pull this thing off, the suffering would be worthwhile.

Another ten minutes passed before he spotted the hairy face emerging from behind a door marked PRIVATE – STAFF ONLY. When the Beard beckoned with his right hand, Morgan made a point of stopping to drain his glass before crossing the room to the staff quarters. The door was locked behind him.

It was a small room, consisting of little more than a couple of easy chairs, a small table and a basic, two-bar electric fire. Waiting in there, aside from the Beard, were the two men involved in the fracas at the flat a week before, looking far from overjoyed to see him, plus one other. It seemed they had brought in reinforcements this time. Morgan allowed himself the briefest of smiles.

"You have a sample of the merchandise, I presume," said the Beard, holding out his hand.

"Of course," replied Morgan, making no move to produce the item, "but I thought I was dealing with the top man this time, not his chief lackey."

The Beard shook his outstretched hand impatiently. "Don't push your luck, Morgan. Let's be sure of what you've got to offer first. Then maybe you get to deal at the top."

Morgan handed over a packet to the Beard, who passed it to the man Morgan had not seen before. Without a word the stranger left, taking the packet with him. Their tests held no fear for the Irishman. The heroin was top quality stuff.

"We've had a bit of an internal problem tonight, that's why we are running a little late," said the Beard. "We're going to have to make a call. Unavoidable, I'm afraid. The tests will take a little while to run, so you can come with us now and after we have attended to our bit of business, we'll work our way back to the lab. Then we shall find out exactly what you are offering us."

Morgan sat in the back of the car very conscious of the bandage wrapped around the wrist of the man beside him; the Beard sat in the front passenger seat while the other man was driving.

"It's time you were formally introduced," decided the Beard, making no effort to conceal the grin that split the mass of hair around his mouth and chin. "This is Lenny, The gentleman driving, believe it or not, is Horace. We choose to call him 'H'. Better for his image, we think."

No words of acknowledgement were exchanged, but then Morgan hardly needed confirmation that he wasn't among friends. He did, however, appreciate the point about the image. Despite the tension of the moment, it was an effort to stifle the urge to laugh. Horace the Heavy; it sounded like something out of a cartoon strip.

When the car pulled up in the kerb, the Irishman tried in vain to pinpoint exactly where they were. Through the gloom of the poorly-lit street he could make out a row of boarded up shops, empty and vandalised, falling into a serious state of disrepair. Further along stood some multi-storey blocks and running away from them an open rubbish-strewn area.

The Beard left the car to have a short meeting with a figure that seemed to materialise out of nowhere and disappear in much the same way.

"Perhaps you would like to join us, Mr. Morgan."

It sounded like more an instruction then an invitation.

Leaving Horace behind the wheel, Morgan was led away by the two others into the dark, open area, stumbling their way between dumped black rubbish bags, torn by animals so that they spilled their contents, old discarded car wheels, rusty bicycle frames and God knows what else.

When he first heard the whimpering, he was unsure whether he had imagined it, except that, as they advanced, it seemed to get louder. It was pitiful, like the crying of a frightened, wounded dog.

Morgan winced as the shaft of light from Lenny's torch carved its way through the darkness. The man lying in a pile of overturned garbage was surely no older than his early twenties. His whole body trembling in unison with the strange, agonised noise that filled the night air, he appeared to be in some sort of delirium in which he had scratched great, red gouges down his face with his own nails. The stench was overpowering as he lay in his own excrement.

"Christ, what a sight," gasped Morgan. "Who the hell is he?"

"One of our distributors."

The Beard's reply showed no trace of emotion. It was a scene he had seen before and would undoubtedly see again.

"You mean a pusher."

"We call them distributors. Has a more professional ring to it."

"Whatever you call him, if he needs a fix so desperately, for Heaven's sake give him one."

Morgan's plea was in vain. The Beard shook his head.

"It's not that simple. He's not short of materials. He gets those as a reward for his services. His commission, if you want to call it that. His problem is getting it inside him. There are so many needle holes in him his veins have collapsed, all over. There's simply nowhere left to put a syringe."

"God, that's awful."

Morgan shuddered. The desperate cries coming up from this whimpering wreck of a man at his feet were getting through to his very soul.

"We'll have to get rid of him."

Morgan couldn't stop himself reacting to what sounded like a death sentence from the Beard.

"What the hell does that mean?" he demanded angrily. "This guy needs proper help and attention."

"Your compassion is commendable, Mr. Morgan, but not very practical," answered the Beard in very matter-of-fact tones. "Although this man is of no further use to us, the last thing we can allow is for him to fall into the hands of the police. He knows too much, knows too many people." Nodding his head in the direction of Lenny, he went on, "Stay with him. When we get back to base, I'll send out some help. And for God's sake shut him up. We'll have the whole bloody neighbourhood down here."

Lenny's fist crashed down on the man's jaw. The whimpering stopped, leaving the air filled with a sudden eerie silence. Morgan wanted desperately to intercede, but had to control his emotions. There was too much at stake. He was too close to blow it now.

"There must be another way."

That weak, final plea was all he could allow himself. Even before he said it, he knew it would fall on deaf ears. It was really little more than a token gesture to help ease his conscience.

"There isn't." As the Beard turned towards Morgan, it was just possible in the torchlight to see the grin flicker across his face, trying to be seen through the mass of wiry hair. Pulling a revolver from inside his coat, he added, "Perhaps you would like to do it for us, Mr. Morgan."

You could almost reach out and touch the silence as the Irishman and the hairy gangster stared coldly at each other over the gun, which rested on the palm of the Beard's outstretched hand.

"I'll not do your dirty work."

"But, Mr. Morgan, I would have thought this was right up your street, shooting a helpless, unarmed man in the back."

The tone was deliberately mocking, designed to fan the flames of hostility that already burned between them.

"In Ireland we are at war."

"I see. So, in the name of war – your word for it, I hasten to add, not mine – you can justify gunning down an unsuspecting, unarmed man leaving church with his wife and kids, but our putting this wretch out of his misery fills you with pious revulsion." The Beard returned the gun to its holster, hidden under his coat. "You're a bloody hypocrite, Mr Morgan. I don't like hypocrites. Neither do I have any time for the so-called cause you fight for. If it was up to me, I would tell you to peddle your wares elsewhere."

"But there's the rub, my furry friend, it isn't up to you is it?"

Morgan knew that rankled. The Beard disliked intensely being seen to have something on his plate too big for him to handle, too important for him to be allowed the final decision. It was obviously a blow to his ego and his image with the men under his command. For Morgan it meant a weakness, the only one, so far as he could see, that he was able to exploit to maintain his position. It was probably the only thing that was keeping him alive.

"You would be well advised not to think of me as your friend, either, Mr. Morgan."

The Irishman was first back to the car, leaning against the wet bodywork as rain began to fall, gasping in deep breaths of cold air. The Beard was only a few seconds behind him.

"What would you like to see now, Mr. Morgan?" he said. "What about a woman? Do you fancy a woman tonight, Mr. Morgan? I could find you one that would do anything for a shot of heroin. And I mean anything. Perform any trick in the book and probably some that aren't. Mind you, you might come away with something you didn't have before you started." He burst into a raucous laugh, which ended abruptly as he continued. "Or perhaps your taste is for the male of the species. I could find you a man who would be equally accommodating for the same price."

"Look, I don't want to hear this," snapped Morgan angrily. "Can we get on and go wherever it is we're going?"

"You shock very easily for one so actively involved in the slaughter of the innocent."

Morgan exploded. "Don't you dare to lecture me about the slaughter of the innocent. Not after what I've seen here tonight."

The Beard grunted derisively. "There are no innocents in this business, Mr. Morgan. The man you've seen tonight is a fool, but he is far from innocent. No-one forced him to put the stuff inside him in the first place. I don't do it. You don't do it. He chose to do it and that was his decision. But it's a habit that costs money. He got hooked beyond his means. The only way he could meet his needs was to deal for us. He knew the risks. Remember, we don't create the demand, we only supply it."

"Your false morality stinks. However much you care to dress it up, we are no different. Don't try to tell me some kid hardly into his teens who starts pill-popping, to experiment or because it's considered trendy, isn't innocent. From there it grows, doesn't it? If people like you didn't ensure the stuff was available, they wouldn't get started so easily. God knows where they find the money to line your filthy pockets. Steal, prostitute their bodies, what do you care?"

"Remember Mr. Morgan, these people you feel so sorry for are going to be lining your filthy pockets. You are quite prepared to provide the means to keep your so-called innocents hooked to fund your campaign to kill and maim."

"Yes, just as the organisation you so dutifully represent is ready to pay to help us to kill and maim your so-called innocents, so that you can continue to get rich plying your filthy trade." Morgan opened the rear door of the car. "And you accuse me of being a hypocrite. You sicken me."

The car journey was dragging on, mainly due to the amount of turning Horace appeared to be doing, seemingly driving around in circles so that Morgan wouldn't know the exact location of their destination. They were wasting their time. He had no idea where they were anyway. The silence was becoming too overbearing for him. He had to break it.

"You're an oddball," he said to the Beard, who had taken the seat beside him now that Lenny had been left behind, "a contradiction. You seem educated, well-bred. It doesn't go with the job."

"You mean what's a nice boy like me doing in a rotten business like this?"

"Something like that," agreed Morgan, "but 'nice' wasn't the word I had in mind. You're a cold, ugly bastard."

"Well, you don't end up in a job like this by answering an ad. in the paper, that's for sure." The Beard paused, looking thoughtfully at the rain that now hammered on the side window. What memories were stirring; how many ifs and what-might-have-beens? "Yes, I had an education, but you meet all types at university. I met what you would probably call the wrong type. I got into trouble, ran up some bad gambling debts; some friends, or so I thought at the time, helped me out. I had to do some favours in return that were not entirely legal. After that I could go only one way."

"You enjoy what you do?"

"Not particularly, but I get well paid for it. There are plenty of people today doing jobs they don't enjoy for the same reason."

"Ah, the money in your pocket justifies all. The pain, the killing, the misery you and your wretched trade inflicts on its unfortunate victims."

"Cut the holier-than-thou crap." The Beard began to show uncharacteristic signs of becoming irritated. "You're about to become part of this wretched trade."

"Not for personal gain," Morgan was quick to point out. "For the cause."

"I piss on your cause."

There was enough of a hint of menace in the way the Beard said that for Morgan to consider it unwise to pursue the conversation further. He also realised he had lost control of his emotions, so coming close to jeopardising everything he was trying to achieve. Lapsing back into silence, the Irishman was in no doubt that he had much to fear from this man who looked more like the traditional image of a captain home from the sea than the purveyor of evil that he was.

Morgan was glad when the journey finally ended. Sitting quietly had served only to give him time to think and he was unable to quell a growing sense of unease that stirred within him. He had become very aware of the loneliness and vulnerability of his position. He was totally at the mercy of this man, whose warped sense of morality saw no wrong in removing from this life a redundant pusher, but was fired with hate and anger at the thought of killing in the name of a political cause. Morgan was sure of only one thing. He was bloody scared.

Dashing through the rain, which continued to hammer down relentlessly, he followed his two travelling companions into a large, detached red-brick house. The Beard instantly disappeared, while Morgan settled uncomfortably on a settee, with only the uncommunicative Horace for company. Why, oh why, did his every instinct tell him to run? Get the hell out of this place and away from these people, not in a minute's time or a few seconds even, but now, this very moment. It was impossible, of course. He had come too far. There could be no turning back.

His fears and apprehensions were accelerated when the Beard returned with three men at his side. Something was happening, but what? There couldn't have been anything wrong with the sample.

"What's the verdict on the goods?" asked Morgan.

"Our lab boys say it's top grade stuff," confirmed the Beard. "There's just one more test we need to make."

"What's that, then?"

The words were hardly out when Horace's arm came around Morgan's neck from behind, squeezing his windpipe in a vice-like grip. He kicked out viciously as the Beard's three comrades descended on him, but a hammer blow to the stomach knocked all the wind out of his body. Gasping, he was thrown heavily to the floor. There was no escape this time. There were too many of them.

Morgan screamed with horror when he saw the full syringe. Holding it up to test the flow, the Beard said. "We're just going to put this little lot inside you. If you are still alive in the morning, I would say you've got a deal."

The Irishman tried to writhe and kick as the Beard came forward, but he was pinned too firmly to the floor. The thought of that massive dose of heroin pouring into his vein filled him with terror and revulsion. Further efforts to resist, as his coat was pulled from him, proved futile. He was never going to succeed against such superior numbers. He became frantic, squirming, yelling.

"No, no, no you crazy bastard," he screamed. "I don't want that stuff inside me."

"Think of the cause, Mr Morgan." The Beard made no attempt to disguise the pleasure this moment was giving him. "All for the good of the cause."

A rubber tube was tightened around Morgan's arm just above the elbow. He felt his veins begin to swell.

"No, no, no!" The screams died on his lips, turning to sobs of helplessness and despair as the needle went in. His last recollection before losing consciousness was of a great wave of nausea sweeping through his body.

Tommy Morgan was soaked through. He lay face-down on the steps outside the front door of the house in which he had his apartment. How long he had been there, he had no idea. His coat had not been put back on him despite the torrential rain. Shivering with the cold and wet, he knew he had to get inside. Otherwise, if he managed to survive the massive heroin overdose, he probably wouldn't survive the pneumonia.

He found the door key in his pocket; reaching the latch was another matter. There was no strength in his limbs. His mind was floating, drifting away from the helpless shell of a body that hauled itself slowly up the rain-soaked door. He had to concentrate, force some semblance of co-ordination between mind and body, but it was such an effort. It would be easier to just lie down in the rain and die.

When the key finally slotted into the lock, the door swung open under his weight and Morgan fell inside. Lying on the floor, exhausted and breathless, he marvelled at the stroke of fortune that had seen him put his door keys in the pocket of his trousers, rather than his coat, when he had left the flat earlier. An involuntary action, seemingly insignificant at the time, done without thought or consideration, may well have saved his life.

He still had to get up the stairs. The darkness was total, yet there was no point in using up valuable strength to haul himself up to reach the light switch. As the cost of the electric to the stair and landing lights was paid for by the owners of the property, the push-in switches were adjusted to pop back out again with the minimum of delay. Even at normal pace, there was barely time to reach the top of the stairs before the light went out.

How long it took him to crawl up, one stair at a time, defying momentary lapses of consciousness, he had no idea. It seemed an age. On reaching the landing at the top, he lay on his back. He could go no further. If he was to die, this is where it would have to be.

A sudden bursting into life of the light forced him to screw up his eyes and turn his head away. The accompanying noise was unmistakeable. Someone was coming up the stairs.

Incredibly, Morgan's muddled, meandering mind registered the fact that it was Friday night. That meant it had to be George. He was later than usual, but there was no-one else it could be. Although Morgan wanted desperately to drag himself out of the way, his body no longer responded to the feeble messages being sent out by his weakening brain. The light would go out as his neighbour made the top of the stairs. The landing switch was beyond where he lay.

And so it was. George's dash ended as he pitched forward on contact with the unseen, inert body spread across his path. In the darkness Morgan could see nothing. But, as he drifted back into the realms of unconsciousness, his ears told him that this was one Friday night George had not made it to the end of the landing on time.

Chapter Ten

Pauline Greenfield sat in a corner seat in the lounge bar of a country pub some ten miles from where she lived. When she had a lunch-time drink with David Maddocks, she always thought it best to be off her own doorstep. People so often came to the wrong conclusions. For the past couple of years she had occasionally had a lunch-time drink with David when her husband was away on trips. It helped break up the loneliness for her, compensate for the lack of contact with other people. How David always seemed to know when her husband was away, she was never really sure. Yet he could always be relied on to telephone as soon as she was alone. Today was different. She had rung David.

Pauline saw nothing wrong with her relationship with David Maddocks, though she did keep it from her husband. To her he was simply a friend. She knew she had too much to lose to even contemplate allowing the relationship to become anything more. She enjoyed the home and comforts her husband's career had brought her. This was, after all, why she had set her sights on him years ago, spotting the potential before it really blossomed.

David lacked her husband's ambition. Although holding a respectable position in the sales department of a local firm, he would never aspire to the same heights. A couple of years younger than her husband, he was taller and more powerfully built. He was a handsome man, charming and fun to be with, but he would never, to quote a cliché, be able to keep her in the manner to which she has become accustomed.

David Maddocks stood at the bar wondering what it was about this woman that made such an impact on him. Certainly she was a good-looking woman, but there was more to it than that. Somewhere there was an extra ingredient that made her just that little bit special.

The moment he had first set eyes on her, preparing for the opening of a charity shop in a small shopping centre close to where he and his then wife, Linda, lived, would live in his memory for ever. The shop was to raise funds to support a nearby, newly opened hospice, a project close to Linda's heart, as her mother had died a few months earlier after a long battle with bowel cancer. She suffered greatly through her final months, but died in a hospital bed, much to Linda's distress, as no adult hospice care was available in the area. Though having no direct criticism of the hospital staff, Linda regretted not being able to find accommodation where her mother could have received more individual care and comfort through her final days. So when plans for a new, local adult hospice entered the public domain, Linda became an enthusiastic, vigorous supporter of the project and was the main driving force behind the opening of the shop. She still worked in the shop and helped out at the hospice.

Pauline was helping to set up displays when David had driven over to the shop in his lunch break the day before the opening, feeling he should show an interest, however forced. The hospice had become something of an obsession for Linda, which he was unable to share. Devoting so much leisure time to the welfare of the sick and the dying did not fit in with his fun-orientated philosophy of life and had created some conflict within the marriage.

Even an old, baggy sweater, looking saggingly a couple of sizes too big for her, and a pair of well-worn, faded jeans, noticeably fraying around the trouser hems, clothes obviously dug out in case she had ended up with a messy job to do, failed to lessen the impact of his first sight of Pauline. He was captivated, not just by the way she looked, but every little movement of her body as he watched her meticulously lift collected, second-hand clothes from a large bag, sort them onto hangers, before placing them as invitingly as possible on a display rail. For him, she was a vision of total and complete perfection. He was unable to take his eyes off her, leading to an awkward moment when Linda became aware of his distraction.

Following that, there looked little chance of approaching Pauline, until Linda, for some reason, unexpectedly retreated to the storeroom at the back of the shop. David seized the opportunity, if only to be close to her for a few seconds. He even managed to talk to her, but only to introduce himself and compliment her on how well she was putting together the display, before the conversation was cut short by a withering look from his wife as she returned to the shop front.

He wasn't sure, and he had thought it better never to ask, how the two had met. Pauline obviously wasn't a close friend of Linda's, as that was the only time he had met her until the chance meeting three years later.

Divorce had come a year or so after the shop opening and David had slipped easily back into the single life. He had a respectable apartment, was capable of looking after himself, comfortable with his own company, but had also dropped happily back into the social scene. Always good company, believing life was there to be enjoyed, he was never short of friends, relishing a busy social life. There had been women too, but nothing serious had developed, possibly because none could bear comparison with the image that had never left his mind of Pauline in the shop that day.

He could think of no way of getting in touch, other than asking his ex-wife, who was unlikely to be forthcoming, so had given up on ever seeing Pauline again, until the evening he walked into a supermarket he never usually frequented.

Despite the years that had passed, he didn't need a second glance to know it was her. The long hair had gone and she was, not surprisingly, dressed differently to their previous encounter, looking so beautiful and elegant in a simple, pale blue dress, coatless in the early summer warmth. The sight of her had no less an effect on him than the moment he had first seen her, setting up a display in the hospice shop, a moment vividly embedded in his mind. He stood there mesmerised, unable to take his eyes off her, as she shuffled along the extensive shelving stacked with variously-priced bottles of wine from countries around the globe. He took in every little movement of her body, every little shifting of her dress, as she reached up to take down bottles, examine the label, and replace on the shelf, unable to choose a preference. He had to grasp the moment. Coming up behind her, as she once more replaced a bottle, he said simply, "Too much choice."

When she turned, a look of surprise was quickly eclipsed by a smile that seemed to light up the whole of her face.

"Hello David." He couldn't believe she had remembered him. It was more than he could have ever hoped for. "Never thought I would bump into you again."

Normally David was not one for platonic relationships with the opposite sex. It simply wasn't his style. If a relationship was slow to go the way he wished it, he usually let it die. Yet, he had never been able to bring himself to do this with Pauline. No woman, not even the wife he was married to for nine years before his divorce, had managed to arouse such desire within him. She dominated his thoughts. Night or day, no matter what he was concentrating on, she would appear. Yet Pauline had never offered him any encouragement. After the first chance meeting, he had visited the supermarket more frequently, on the same day around the same time, and the encounters had become more frequent. Eventually there followed a coffee in the store restaurant, moving on to the occasional lunch-time or afternoon drink, usually when her husband was away on business trips. David had a wide circle of friends, including one who worked for the travel agency that booked all business travel and accommodation for Impact Publicity Services, so he was privy to information on her husband's travel arrangements. Throughout, Pauline had never given any indication that, while she enjoyed his company, allowing him some leeway with his flirtatious comments, she would let the relationship to develop into anything more. In his mind he had possessed this woman's body a thousand times. In reality, she was unattainable. He preferred not to dwell on how much that fanned the desire.

Returning to the table with the drinks, he sat as close beside her as he was able without censure. The longing to reach out and touch her had to be resisted. That surely would be a wrong move, almost certainly bringing an end to their relationship, such as it was. He enjoyed being with her too much to risk that. Also, of course, while he continued to see her as a friend, there was always a glimmer of hope, however remote, of it drifting into something deeper. Had she not telephoned him this morning? She had never done that before.

"I would like to believe you rang me because you couldn't go another day without seeing me," said David, sipping his gin and tonic, "but I expect I would be deluding myself."

Pauline smiled. "David, you know I like to see you, but yes, there was more to today's 'phone call than that. I desperately need to talk to someone."

The events of the previous evening had left Pauline greatly distressed. Alone in the house that morning, she had been overcome with a need to unload her anxieties onto someone, try to make sense of it all. With her only family a sister who lived sixty miles away, it had to be David. He was the only friend she had. She had drifted away from the friends she knew before her marriage and had built up no new ones except David.

"So you weren't overcome with a sudden urge of lust for my body," said David, with an exaggerated sigh.

"Please David, just for once, let's be serious," snapped Pauline. "I'm not in the mood for this nonsense."

She immediately regretted her reprimand. When they had first started to meet, he had made no secret of what he was looking for in their relationship, but she had treated his propositions light-heartedly. Now they were treated as a standing joke between them, yet there remained just enough of an undercurrent of seriousness about them to please her. Howard never said anything to make her feel desirable or beautiful. A woman needed that sometimes.

There were times when she felt guilty about using David. She didn't need actual physical fulfilment, the look of longing she caught occasionally in his eye being enough, so it was possible their meetings were somewhat frustrating for him. So long as he continued to see her, she presumed he was content.

"David, I'm desperately worried about Howard."

"Good Lord, have you brought me here to talk about Howard?" He raised his hands at her instant reproving look. "All right, I'm sorry. What's Howard been up to?"

She poured out the whole story, from the dubious accounting for the frightening lump on the back of his skull on returning from Barcelona to the drunken end of the previous evening. David listened in silence, staring intently at the pithy slice of lemon floating on top of his drink.

"Pauline, what do you want me to say?" he said at the conclusion of her report. "That it makes some sort of sense to me?"

"Not really, I suppose." There was a sad note of resignation. "That would have been nice, but was too much to hope for. I think I just needed someone to unload it on instead of bottling it up inside."

"Well, at least I've done that much for you."

David found it hard to sympathise with Pauline's obvious concern for her husband, his desire for her overriding all other emotions. From the outside, her marriage to Howard had seemed perfect. She had always seemed to be content. From the start she had made it clear they were nothing more than friends, so that David's attempts to turn their relationship into something deeper had become futile. God knows what Howard was up to, but he may well have made the first move for him. Suddenly there was a hint of vulnerability about Pauline. Could the ball really be drifting into his court?

"Look, I don't think you should go back to your empty house this afternoon," he suggested. "How would you like to go down to the park?"

"Isn't it a bit cold for that?"

"We've got our coats. It'll do more good than sitting in that empty house brooding all afternoon."

Pauline's face brightened considerably. Although known locally as the park, that was not really what it was. It was a section of woodland cut into two by a fast-running stream, a spot Pauline loved. She had only been once or twice before with David, but went often on her own, particularly in the summer.

"Don't you have to go back to work?" she asked.

David shrugged. "I'll ring in; tell them I've been stricken by a mystery illness during lunch."

Watching him walk away to make the telephone call, Pauline sat back and relaxed for the first time that day. Somehow she couldn't see Howard telephoning the office in the middle of the day to feign sickness so that he could be with her. But then that was probably a reflection of why her husband had risen to be a senior executive while David would never be more than a senior clerk in a sales department. And she did enjoy the lifestyle Howard's position afforded.

Leaving her Metro on the pub car park, she joined David in his car for the short, ten-minute drive to the local beauty spot. Even the harshness of winter couldn't dim the appeal this place held for Pauline. There were enough evergreens surrounding the stream to neutralise the stark effect of the bare, outstretched, twisted branches on the trees that shed their load through the autumn days.

They walked for a while on the carpet of rotting, yellow leaves that covered the banks, past the little wooden tea hut that in summer would be open, back to the rickety wooden bridge that spanned the fast-flowing water. Standing on the creaky boards, watching the stream rush past below her, spray lightly brushing her face, the fresh breeze biting into her cheeks, here was a peace so complete she could put her worries behind her. They belonged to another world, an ugly world, far removed from the beauty around her.

"Feeling better now?" asked David. He had moved so close to her, their bodies were faintly touching.

She turned her face to his. "This was just what I needed. I don't know what I would do without you sometimes."

She had plenty of time to avoid the kiss. He lowered his head slowly, as though expecting her to turn away. But at that moment in time, at that place, the tranquillity disturbed only by the soothing sound of rushing water, the real world left behind, kissing David seemed the most natural thing to do.

For Pauline it was not a sexual kiss. It was more a search for comfort and reassurance, as a troubled child would look to a mother's arms for solace. Not until David slightly increased the pressure on her lips, gently easing open her mouth, did the full implication of what she was doing hit her. Breaking off the kiss, she violently pushed herself away from David's grasp.

"That was stupid," she cried loudly. "Stupid! Stupid! Stupid!"

The anger was with herself for what she considered a moment of weakness. Knowing how David truly felt about her, she should not have allowed herself a moment of such vulnerability. The last thing she needed at the moment was an affair. She was sure the answer to her problems didn't lie between another man's sheets. Her wish was for her marriage to survive, though, if she were honest with herself, it was impossible to say if this was because she loved her husband or desperately wanted to preserve the way of life she had become used to.

For the second time in a matter of hours Pauline found herself travelling in a car with a man in complete silence. This time she blamed herself. Had she not taken that extra bit of care getting ready that morning? Had she not put on the pale blue dress that she knew David liked? Howard's behaviour had evoked feelings of neglect and rejection, so that she had looked to David in her need to be aware again of her appeal as a woman. She had only wanted to see it in his eyes, though, feel it in his presence, never going so far as a kiss. She was a parasite, she decided, drawing strength off this man's deepest feelings. It would probably be best if she never saw him again.

After dropping Pauline back at the pub car park, David returned to his office, much to the surprise of colleagues who were under the impression he had been struck by a sudden attack of violent diarrhoea during the lunch hour.

Back at his desk, he picked up the telephone and spoke to Angela on the switchboard.

"Does Ross Hankin still work at our Spanish agency?"

"To the best of my knowledge; in Madrid."

"See if you can get him for me, will you?"

"It'll take a few minutes. I'll call you back."

Returning the receiver to the telephone, David leaned back in his chair, contemplating the afternoon's events. The kiss had surprised him, never having come remotely close to that before. She had always been a brick wall to his advances and propositions. He closed his eyes and recalled the touch of her lips on his, the closeness of her body. For a few fleeting seconds on that bridge the agonisingly unattainable had suddenly seemed wildly attainable. He had tasted the fruit and it was as sweet as he had imagined. Now he had to pick the tree clean.

The ring of the telephone broke into his thoughts. Russ Hankin had worked with David for many years before moving to Spain, during which time they had become good friends.

After exchanging pleasantries, David came to the point.

"Tell me, Russ, do you have such things as private detectives out there?"

"Of course we do," answered the voice from Spain. "Believe it or not, we even have electricity and running water out here too."

David laughed. "All right, I take your point. I want you to hire a detective for me. Personal, not business, so have the bill sent to me direct. This is what I want him to check out for me."

Chapter Eleven

Throughout his working life, Jason G Henderson, Managing Director of Impact Publicity Services, had rigidly believed there was no greater folly than to get involved with a female office colleague. Invariably, such relationships ended only in marriage or heartache and he wasn't sure which was the most painful.

His own unhappy, ten-year marriage had come to a sudden end some twenty years before, when his wife collapsed one afternoon while shopping in Oxford Street, dying three hours later in hospital without coming out of the coma. Doctors had found a massive brain tumour that had lain dormant for years, undetected. Sooner or later it was going to activate and take her life. Her fate had been inevitable.

In spite of knowing how callous and cruel the thought was, Henderson couldn't help wishing it had been sooner. For him it had come as nothing but a great relief, a heavy burden removed from his shoulders. Pushed into marriage by family pressure in what was considered a 'proper' match, they were, in fact, the epitome of incompatibility. Their tastes opposite on virtually every facet of their lives, they agreed on nothing, argued about everything. Her fiery temper frequently led to wild tantrums when she would smash crockery, ornaments or anything else she was able to lay her hands on. These rages were frightening and so intense Henderson always felt she was capable of killing when consumed by them. After her death he had asked the doctors if the dormant tumour could have had any effect on her mental state, but none seemed to be able to come to a definite conclusion.

That they continued in a marriage, when it would have made sense to have parted years before, was due entirely to the enormous pressure within their social circle at that time. For their class separation and divorce was unthinkable.

So he suffered until fate took a hand, snuffing out a life only a few weeks away from the completion of its thirty-first year.

In nearly twenty-years since then, he had had little to do with the opposite sex. Much embittered by his wretched marital experience, he had been content to live out a bachelor existence, needing to please only himself, answerable to no-one.

He was sure his self-imposed discipline regarding office relationships had gone a long way to preserving his independence. Into his fifties and looking every minute his age, he hardly gave it a thought now, sure that temptation was well and truly behind him. Events proved such complacency ill-founded. But when she arrived on the scene, who would have guessed Devina would be the one to prove him wrong?

Certainly Henderson had never encountered anyone like her in a working environment and that was not meant in a complimentary way. If the decision had been his, her appearance alone would have lost her the job, irrespective of her capabilities or qualifications. Group Personnel, however, had told him he was old-fashioned and out-of-touch. Given the chance, he felt Group Personnel would replace him with some long-haired trendy in baggy jumper, jeans and trainers! The modern image, they would say.

Devina, Henderson had checked, was nineteen years of age and, though not much over five feet tall, would certainly not go unnoticed. She wore tight tops, tight leather mini-skirts that bordered on the indecent together with, usually, fishnet tights. Her lipstick, always matching her finger and toe nail varnish, came in a variety of shades of purple, black and very dark red. To Henderson her hair looked as though it hadn't seen a comb for a week, yet he was assured it took more than an hour every morning to achieve that look.

Jason Henderson found it all curiously sexless. It was too blatant, too obvious. All of which made subsequent events all the more surprising.

The morning his secretary went down with influenza, it left him with a problem. Summoning Howard Greenfield to his office, he paused to reflect how much he had come to rely on Howard since the slight heart attack three years previously. The fact that he was in hospital only a few days and away from the office for about six weeks did not, the doctors had said, entitle him to just shrug off the attack. Take it as a warning, they had advised; ease up or face the possibility of more serious consequences. That was why he allowed Greenfield to take most of the creative and client liaison responsibilities off his shoulders, leaving him to deal solely with the administrative running of the company.

"Howard, I've got a problem," declared Henderson. "As you know, Marje has gone down with flu and the Group Chairman has called an emergency board meeting at the Metropole in Brighton."

Greenfield raised his eyebrows. "What's that all about?"

"Officially the marked decline in Group profitability, as revealed in the latest trading figures."

"That doesn't apply to us surely. I would have thought our profits were up."

"They are, but the Group does carry some lame ducks, unfortunately." Henderson began to smile. "I shouldn't read too much into it, Howard. It's really just an excuse for a large-scale executive booze-up; a night out with the boys. Nevertheless, I do like to keep an accurate record of such meetings and it would appear that, next to Marjorie, young Devina has the fastest shorthand speed. Over a hundred words a minute, would you believe, and the certificates to prove it. What's your impression, Howard?"

Greenfield sat back in his chair. "I can well believe her shorthand speed. She seems to be very good at her job."

"You say that as though there's an unmentioned 'but'."

Greenfield shrugged. "Her appearance is a little startling, Jason, to say the least."

"I know," Henderson sighed. "I wasn't very keen, but Group Personnel thought it would up-date our image. Image is very much the in-thing at the moment. We have to present a modern image, whatever that is, to the client"

"It may please some; not all though."

"Try telling that to those weirdoes with their sociology degrees that have taken over Group Personnel. They seem to think if you have long, straggly hair, dress and look generally scruffy or outrageous, then you must be a genius."

Greenfield laughed. "I think that's a slight exaggeration."

Getting up from his chair, Henderson walked over to the window, looking out aimlessly at the traffic passing by.

"Maybe so, but times do seem to have changed such a lot in this business since we started, Howard. I feel sometimes I'm being left behind."

"Don't despair, Jason. It's just one of the drawbacks of getting older."

Henderson turned and smiled. "Yes, I suppose you could be right. I am sounding off a bit, aren't I?"

"Spit it all out, it's good for you."

"Yes, and you are a good listener, Howard." Henderson returned to his desk. "Anyway, back to the business in hand. You think Devina could stand in for Marje at this meeting?"

"After twenty years of Marjorie she'll probably come as a bit of a shock to your colleagues, but I don't doubt she is capable."

"She may not wish to come, of course. It will mean a stop-over."

"I can't see that being a problem. Night out at a five-star hotel? I would think she would jump at the chance."

She did, too. The board meeting went exactly as Henderson had predicted. After a brief, unproductive exchange of views, there was a mass adjournment to the lounge bar. While providing something of a distraction to some of the directors, Devina appeared to have no problems recording the discussion.

No longer keen, since his illness, on excessive alcohol, Henderson excused himself and his stand-in secretary from the proceedings shortly after eleven. He was tired and ready for bed. Devina accompanied him to the second floor, where they departed to their separate rooms.

After relaxing in a piping hot bath, he put on his striped, cotton pyjamas and was about to pull back the covers when there was a knock on the door.

"Who is it?" Henderson was undoubtedly cautious at that time of night.

"Devina."

"Devina? Are you all right?"

"Sure, I'm okay. Just let me in please."

Convinced there must be something wrong, Henderson quickly slipped on his plain, brown dressing gown and opened the door. Devina swept in, a full-length kimono-style dressing gown, flaunting vivid, colourful designs, wrapped around her. From the way her body moved within the silky, clinging material, it was obvious she was wearing nothing beneath it. For the first time she evoked a physical reaction within him.

"I'm sorry, I'm being silly, I know," she said ruefully.

"Not at all. What is it?"

"It's just hotel rooms. Especially when they are as big as these are. I find them such lonely places." She looked deep into Henderson's eyes. "Don't you?"

He shut the door and locked it.

Jason Henderson couldn't fathom out why he had broken his long-standing rule for this girl, still not out of her teens, who had hovered around the office in tight mini-skirts and fishnet tights without inducing any sexual reaction in him. In the dim light of a bedside lamp, he lay back pondering with concern his lapse. He should have been stronger, sent her away. Now he could foresee only problems. Where did it go from here? Devina slept soundly, her naked shoulders just showing above the covers. The dazzling kimono lay draped across the lower half of the bed.

What were her motives? He was more than thirty years older than she and looked his age, if not older. Could she really find him sexually attractive? Perhaps she thought sleeping with the Managing Director would further her career. That was where his problems could really begin. He cursed his moment of indiscretion.

Not that it hadn't been a pleasant experience. He had long forgotten the vigour and urgency of the lovemaking of youth, the consuming eagerness of those early years of awakening and discovery. But it had left him exhausted. Even now he was having trouble getting his breath. His pulse was still racing, seemingly throbbing through his whole body.

Closing his eyes, he looked to sleep to recover his strength and relieve his anxieties. He never opened his eyes again. The physical exertion had proved too much for his imperfect heart. Devina slept on, unaware that death was now her bed-mate.

Chapter Twelve

David Maddocks shook his head in disbelief at the report, submitted most efficiently in English, from the Spanish private investigations agency. So it really was true. Though the information was sparse, it was surely conclusive.

A young woman had collected Howard Greenfield in the early evening. He had not returned to his hotel until close to daybreak. Only a few hours later the same woman had picked him up again.

It still left a lot unexplained. Why was he still acting strangely, as Pauline had indicated? A two-day fling in a foreign city might induce an immediate feeling of guilt, but surely he would have recovered to some degree by now. Of course, it could be more than a two-day fling. But if it was someone he knew in London and the trip abroad had been used as an opportunity to be together, why had they not spent the night in the same hotel room?

The agency had been unable to trace anything of Greenfield's movements in Barcelona, save his business appointments, which were hardly a secret anyway. In view of there being no immediate prospect of progress in this direction, they felt, according to the covering letter accompanying the report, it was unfair to continue to take his money.

David was unhappy the trail had petered out. There was so much still unanswered. However, while not the stuff private eye movies are made of, he had to admire their honesty. In truth, it had been the barrel of a gun pointed at a head, rather than integrity that had persuaded the agency to terminate their enquiries.

The telephone at the other end of the line rang on and on. David was about to give up when Pauline answered.

"Pauline, it's David."

Her sigh was loud enough to be clearly heard down the telephone line.

"David, please leave me alone. I don't want you to ring me."

"I think we should meet. I have something to show you that may have some bearing on Howard's behaviour."

"Tell me over the phone."

"I don't think I should. It's something you should see for yourself."

"Then forget it, David." She was adamant. "I think seeing you would be very unwise. I've got more than I can handle with Howard at the moment. I don't need any more problems."

"No change with Howard then."

"Worse, if anything." After a pause, she added, "Look David, you're a nice guy and the last thing I want is to hurt you, but please leave me alone. Don't spoil the friendship we had by becoming a nuisance and making me hate you for it."

Before he could answer she had replaced the receiver. Slipping the report back into its envelope, he dropped it into the top drawer of his desk. He could wait. He was sure now his moment would come.

Chapter Thirteen

Tommy Morgan had lost two days of his life. Sitting over a mug of strong coffee, his desperate efforts to recall anything since the needle was plunged into his arm stirred nothing more than vague images of torrential rain and a slow, painful crawl up the stairs in the darkness. He had no idea how he managed to get into his flat even, the most likely answer being that his neighbour, George, had dragged him there. His ageing battery radio, through the crackles, told him it was Sunday evening.

The mess he found himself lying in appalled him. Despite his comatose state for two days, it would appear his bodily functions had continued as usual. There was also vomit on the floor beside him. The stench from him and the room was overpowering.

While washing himself down and cleaning the room as best as he could, Morgan had wondered how close he had been to death. He guessed it was probably only that he was young and fit that had enabled him to survive. It was impossible to imagine what these people had hoped to achieve by pumping him full of such a massive overdose of heroin. Perhaps they felt that treating him so roughly would give them a psychological advantage when it came to negotiating a deal. Obviously, they would be out to knock down the price. It could be they considered a display of their ability to inflict suffering and pain on him gave them a position of power from which to do this.

Now, sipping his hot coffee, a more sinister thought struck Morgan. It may be the Beard hated him and the cause he represented to such an extent he simply derived a sadistic pleasure from causing him suffering to the point of pushing him to the very brink of death.

Whether it was that thought or the intense cold of the room that made him shiver he wasn't sure. The small, upright paraffin heater fought a losing battle against the accumulated cold of two heatless days and nights.

Morgan jumped at the knock on the door. What was happening to him? Were his nerves really so shattered? How he longed for it to be all over. How much he wanted to simply go home.

"Who's there?"

"Well, you are alive after all." There was no mistaking the voice. "You know who it is Mr. Morgan. Open up please."

The Beard was alone this time. Presumably, it was considered the Irishman would be in no state to constitute a physical threat.

"You know we have a front door downstairs that is supposed to be our security in here," Morgan observed. "You people seem to come and go through it as you please."

"Please Mr. Morgan, don't insult us," smiled the Beard. "Remember who you are dealing with. I only knock at this door out of courtesy."

"You seem determined I shouldn't forget who I am dealing with."

"Ah, you're referring to our little experiment the other night. We had to be sure we weren't going to kill anyone. At least, not until they've had enough to make it worthwhile." The Beard gave the dirty, untidy apartment a disparaging look. "God, this place really is disgusting. And it stinks too. Open a bloody window for Christ's sake."

Morgan's anger boiled over. That this man could treat so lightly the abuse he had inflicted upon his body was more than he could bear. Springing forward, he pinned the Beard against the damp, peeling wallpaper that seemed to be losing its desperate battle to cling to the wall. This time surprise was on the Irishman's side. Before the Beard could react, Morgan's hand darted inside his coat, relieved the shoulder holster of its snub-nosed revolver and pushed the barrel up into the mass of hair covering the underside of his chin.

"Do you know why this room stinks?" Morgan had never known an emotion so strong as the hate he felt for this man. What a service to humanity he would perform by pulling the trigger here and now. "It stinks because I have been out for two days on this floor thanks to you, crapping and pissing in my clothes where I lay, piling up vomit beside me. When I finally opened my eyes, my head was resting in the vomit, can you imagine that? Can you imagine what it's like to feel your hair matted with sick? You did that to me. God knows how close I came to dying."

The Beard remained calm and unruffled in the face of the Irishman's frenzy. "But you haven't died have you, Mr. Morgan, you have survived. And think what a contribution you are making to the cause. You'll go back to Ireland a hero. They'll probably make you a saint."

Morgan rammed the gun barrel hard against the underside of the Beard's jaw, clattering his head back against the wall. The rage that consumed him was close to running out of control.

"You know there is nothing I would like more right now than to blow your head clean off your shoulders."

"Do you think I'm scared of jumped-up punks like you?"

Suddenly there was a spark of defiance about the Beard as he fixed Morgan with a stare from cold, slate-grey eyes full of contempt. "You haven't got the belly for it. Your lot murders by proxy, a bomb left in a street, in a shop or a pub, so that you can be long gone when the blood and guts begin to fly."

"We use guns often enough."

"Oh, sure. On a soldier with his back to you or some off-duty copper sitting unsuspecting in his car yards away." Morgan pulled back the hammer with a click that seemed to echo around the room, but there was no sign of fear from the Beard. "Can you look a man in the eye and pull the trigger, that is the question. Have you that sort of guts, Mr. Morgan? I don't think you have."

The two men stared hard into each other's eyes, the Beard's look throwing out a challenge, daring the Irishman to prove him wrong by carrying out his threat. All it needed was the slightest squeeze on the trigger, the tiniest movement of the finger.

The Beard allowed himself the flicker of a smile. "As I thought, Mr. Morgan, no guts. Just not bloody man enough, are you?"

Easing back the hammer, Morgan turned away, venting his anger and frustration by hurling the gun across the room.

"Besides," the Beard went on, "blowing me to Kingdom come wouldn't please your masters, would it? You came here to make a deal." Crossing the room to retrieve his revolver, he wrinkled his nose disapprovingly. "This place really does stink. How do you live in this doss-hole?"

He pushed open a window, allowing the freezing wind to rush in, instantly wiping out the feeble efforts of the paraffin heater to penetrate the cold of the room.

"I hope I won't have to much longer." Morgan rubbed together his hands as he bent over the heater. "I have a home across the water. I would like to be back there by Christmas."

"And so you shall be. I am the bearer of good news. Glad Christmas tidings, if you like. Yet look at the welcome I get."

"Oh, do forgive me. Next time you almost kill me with an armful of junk, I'll roll out the red carpet."

The Beard was unable to suppress a laugh. "You are excitable this morning. You should be pleased. You're alive and that's clinched your deal. Or, at least, the chance to negotiate."

"There's nothing to negotiate. The price wasn't negotiable to start with and, after what I have been through, it certainly isn't negotiable now. You are getting a bargain and you know it."

"We shall see."

"When shall we see? When do I get to meet your top man?"

"Friday night. In the Mole with Two Heads, as before. Be there about eight thirty."

Morgan looked surprised. "A crowded pub on a Friday night. Isn't that a bit conspicuous?"

"On the contrary, we're far less likely to be noticed in that situation. I will be there before you. When you arrive, join me at my table. The man you want to see will join us shortly after your arrival."

"I'll be there. I just want to get this over with and go home."

The Beard hesitated at the door. "Do I detect a weakening in the commitment to the cause?" There was no mistaking the mocking tone. "Surely it is all worth it, Mr. Morgan."

"For God's sake get out of here," bawled Morgan, "I should have blown your head off when I had the chance."

"It takes a man to do a man's job."

The Beard stepped out onto the landing. Morgan kicked the door shut behind him.

He began to shiver. After turning up the paraffin heater to its highest setting, he slammed shut the window.

Chapter Fourteen

"Did old Henderson really snuff it while he was on the job?"

Greenfield surveyed the gangling youth, seemingly still battling with the teenage traumas of acne, standing before him and wondered whatever happened to innocence. When he had become the junior member of the firm more than twenty-five years before, a shy, hesitant refugee from a sheltered, cosseted upbringing, he would barely have understood the rumours sweeping the office about the demise of their Managing Director. How did this change come about, whereby modern youth knew and talked openly of facets of life he, at their age, even if he understood, could not have mentioned without an obvious reddening of the face?

"For Heaven's sake, Graham. Show a little respect."

The reprimand proved a wasted gesture.

"I don't see why I should particularly," replied the youth. "I didn't like him very much and he certainly didn't have much time for me."

"He was a busy man, Graham."

It was amazing sometimes how an untruth could roll so quickly and easily, instinctively almost, off the tongue. However, the gasp of derision it drew from the young man indicated he was far from convinced.

"We're not blind, Mr Greenfield. We all know you have been running the company more than he has in recent times."

Greenfield shrugged. "He was not a well man."

Exactly why he was sitting there making excuses to the office junior for the behaviour of the Managing Director, he couldn't really fathom. The man had been dead for three days, anyway. Yet the lack of respect and absence of tolerance in the youth's crude manner riled him, but the excuses were falling on deaf ears.

"Then he should have found quieter pastimes than screwing the deadly Devina,"protested Graham. "What a way to go though, eh? Strange combination, mind you. Wouldn't really have thought she was his type, or vice-versa, would you, Mr. Greenfield?"

"What I think is that you must have some work to do. I suggest you curtail your lurid thoughts and get on with it."

Disappointed at not getting confirmation of the stories flying around on the Managing Director's sudden passing, Graham left Greenfield's office to return to the boredom of his daily mundane tasks. What he didn't know was that Greenfield was in no position to confirm or deny the rumoured circumstances of Jason Henderson's death. It didn't sound much like the man he knew. Yet it was odd that Devina had not returned to work or made any contact since the trip to Brighton. Not even a telephone call. Greenfield had heard nothing more than the speculation everyone else appeared to have heard.

Despite their relationship being more a business one than a social one, Henderson's death had come as a shock. Greenfield rarely mixed with work colleagues outside the office environment, unless on official company business, yet a bond of friendship can grow quite strongly between people who work closely together over a long period of time. It was difficult to reconcile the fact that this man, who had been part of his everyday life for so many years, was gone. The permanence of it had not yet really sunk in. He still half expected to see Henderson appear in the doorway, bellowing his customary loud "Good morning" to one and all as he swept through to his office.

The telephone bell interrupted his increasingly morbid train of thought.

"Sir Kenneth and two other gentlemen have just arrived, Mr. Greenfield, I thought you would like to know." It was the voice of Sandra in Reception. "They are in Mr. Henderson's office."

Mr. Henderson's office, she had said. For how long would they go on calling it Mr. Henderson's office? How long would they go on referring to Jason Henderson as though he was still there?

No matter how he tried to keep himself busy with the work spread across his desk, Greenfield couldn't help reflecting on why Sir Kenneth Craig and the others were there. The communication which advised of their coming had done so without giving any indication as to the purpose of the visit, though it was fair to assume it was connected with the sudden loss of Jason Henderson. The Chairman of the board of the Ibex Holdings Group of Companies was not known for social visits to the offices of Impact Publicity Services. It was late morning before Greenfield was summoned to the Managing Director's office.

Sir Kenneth Craig, a short, plump man with grey, thinning hair, complemented by a bushy moustache of the same colour, sucking constantly on a pipe that never seemed to be alight, gestured to him to be seated. Introducing Mr. Follett, the group Personnel Director, and Mr. Carthew, the other board member present, Sir Kenneth, after an obligatory clearing of the throat, began to speak.

"Mr. Greenfield, you have no doubt deduced we are here in connection with the tragic and sudden death of Mr. Henderson. It must also be true that you have heard the rumours circulating with regard to the circumstances of his death. Please understand that what I am about to tell you is in the strictest confidence and must be treated accordingly." There was a pause as Sir Kenneth appeared to give some thought as to the exact form of words to use. "Believe it or not, the rumours you have heard are true. Mr Henderson did die from a heart attack brought on by exhaustive sexual activity with another employee of the company."

Greenfield was stunned. So that really was how it had happened. Suddenly Graham's crudeness didn't seem so out of place.

Sir Kenneth continued, "We on the board are most anxious that the truth of this matter should not become public knowledge. We will even issue a denial, if necessary. Devina Hart, of course, will not be returning to our employment. It is neither her wish nor ours that she should do so. What we want more than anything now is to keep it out of the newspapers. It might make juicy reading for devotees of certain sections of the national press, but for us, we feel, even if we publicly deny it, untold damage could be done to our reputation and client-relationships."

"We have had no enquiries from the press here so far."

"Nevertheless, Mr. Greenfield, I think we must accept the possibility of some of the rumours in circulation filtering through."

"Jason, er Mr. Henderson, built up some strong relationships with the press over the years. He has a lot of friends out there, enough possibly to keep the sordid details out of print."

"Am I to believe you are talking about honour on Fleet Street?" The Chairman of the board was hugely sceptical.

"Don't knock it, Sir Kenneth," advised Greenfield, "it's all you've got. Personally, I think it will be enough."

"We can only hope so. Certainly Miss Hart has been well looked after, so we are not anticipating any problems there."

Sir Kenneth leaned forward on the desk, twirling the inactive pipe irritatingly in his hands. "Anyway, we must move on to the main reason for our visit here today, namely the question of Mr. Henderson's replacement. As you probably know, he was looking to retire in the next few years and in view of that had already made certain recommendations to the board. The crux of these, Mr. Greenfield, was that by that time you would be the most suitable person to succeed him."

Greenfield's heart began to race. Was this finally the moment he had striven so hard for over the years? But what was the implication of the phrase "by that time?" Did that mean he wasn't considered to be ready? If someone else was appointed now, around the same age perhaps or just a little older, it would signal the end of his long-held hopes and aspirations. He would never become head of the firm. His ultimate ambition would never be realised.

Sir Kenneth continued, "We have given this matter considerable thought and discussed it at great length, reviewing all of Mr. Henderson's comments and recommendations, many of which we have down in writing." Unable to conceal his eager anticipation, Greenfield moved to the edge of his seat. How he wished he could hurry the man along. "The board feels it is important that this upset causes minimum disturbance. Normality should be resumed as soon as possible. The agency has a fair number of big-money accounts, which must suffer no fall off in service, however temporary. After due consideration, therefore, we felt there was nothing to be gained from advertising the post and going outside. We have every confidence, Mr. Greenfield, in offering you the position as Managing Director of Impact Publicity Services."

Only the certainty that it would be frowned on in present company stopped Howard Greenfield from leaping into the air. Although more in keeping with the rules of decorum, the smile of deep satisfaction he allowed himself hardly reflected the joy he felt. Here it was, the culmination of more than twenty-five years' dedication to the company, the fulfilling of an ambition that had motivated his daily life since the times when he went uncomplainingly about the dogsbody jobs that Graham now constantly bemoaned. Did this youngster have such lofty aspirations? Somehow, Greenfield doubted it.

"I am flattered by your confidence in me, Sir Kenneth. I shall do my best to ensure it has not been misplaced."

It was said only because it was the right thing to say. Greenfield had no doubts he could do the job.

"We are sure we are doing the right thing. The board's decision was unanimous," Sir Kenneth went on. "Mr. Follett will fill you in on how this change of status affects your job details, such as pension rights and, most importantly of course, your salary. Furthermore, your new position entitles you to a place on the board of Ibex Holdings, so we look forward to seeing you at future meetings." Sir Kenneth got to his feet, obviously ready to take his leave from the proceedings. "I have another appointment, which I am not going to make if I don't get a move on. I will have to leave you in the capable hands of Mr. Follett."

Offering his hand, which Greenfield shook vigorously, the chairman of Ibex Holdings added, "Good luck, Mr. Greenfield – or rather Howard now you are one of us. I shall be back this afternoon. We will get the staff together around, say three-thirty, and I will make a formal announcement. Get in a drop of champagne, perhaps make a bit of an occasion of it. May help to give everyone a lift after the shock of the suddenness of Mr. Henderson's death."

As soon as he was free, Greenfield telephoned Pauline to ask her to come up to the city for lunch. They had a favourite restaurant just off the Strand and they agreed to meet at one o'clock.

It was a cold, gloomy, early-December day, but London was alive with the hustle and bustle of Christmas shoppers. Normally he hated the thronging crowds, yet today nothing could dampen his mood. Pauline was already seated at a table when he arrived at the restaurant, though he was dead on time. He had seemed so different on the telephone to the way he had been for the past two months or so, she had rushed in, eager to find out what had inspired the change.

Greenfield watched her as she pondered over the large menu, remembering the days when he first knew her and had made so many excuses to go to the typing pool to see her. True the long waist-length hair he had found so irresistible had gone, replaced by a short, close-cut style she had considered more suitable as she grew older. Yet this had added a hint of maturity which, strangely, had made her appearance more attractive to him, rather than less.

His spirits were soaring, the adrenalin flowing freely through his veins stimulating all his senses, so that her mere presence was enough to arouse him considerably. He wanted so much to make love to her, there and then, but was sure that such public display of exhilaration would not be welcomed by the patrons of such a high-class establishment!

"So, what's the occasion?" asked Pauline, leaning her elbows on the table, cradling a glass of white wine in her fingers.

"I have some news I thought you would like to hear."

Greenfield was deliberately stalling, teasingly prolonging the agony.

"Well, come on then, don't keep me hanging on for ever."

Pauline laughed. It was good to see him so alive and buoyant again after the stress and strain of recent weeks. The sparkle was back in his eye, the lilt back in his voice. Although she hardly dared believe it, there seemed a real possibility that the misery which had hung over them since his trip to Barcelona, depressingly dominating their lives and filling her with so much fear and anxiety, was over at last.

"Your husband is the new Managing Director of Impact Publicity Services."

The gasp of delight was for her husband's benefit, as the news didn't come as too much of a surprise to her. She had always known this day would come. Jason Henderson's death had served only to bring it a little sooner than she had expected. None of this, however, did anything to lessen her joy, as she put down her glass and leaned across to fleetingly kiss his lips. An intoxicating feeling of relief flooded through her. Surely this meant and end to the pain and torment of the past two months. Today was a new beginning for them.

"Congratulations. No wonder you look so pleased with yourself."

In a way it was the culmination of many years' dedication for Pauline, also. Seeing his potential within days of arriving in the typing pool at Impact Publicity Services, she had picked him out as her best chance of living the sort of life she saw for herself. Although he always felt it was he who did the chasing, in reality he was ever the prey and she the hunter. Yet, throughout the years of marriage, she considered she had played her part in furthering his career, making him happy and providing him with a good home, creating a personal peace of mind that left him free to concentrate wholly on succeeding at work. She had not been disappointed in the rewards this success had brought her.

Pauline had never pretended to herself that she had loved Howard Greenfield when she became his wife. It was something which had never been important in her scheme of things – until now. Recent events had examined her emotions in a way never previously experienced, as the marriage she had so carefully nurtured threatened to crumble into dust at her feet. What were her real feelings? Had she fallen in love with him over the years? Was such a thing really possible? Or was it the life being married to him had given her she had fallen in love with? Whichever way, she saw it as something she desperately wanted to preserve.

"I'm sorry to have dragged you all the way up here," said Greenfield, "but I was bursting to tell you and wanted to see the look on your face. There are times when the telephone is too impersonal."

"I'm glad you did, Howard. I wouldn't have missed sharing this moment with you for the world," smiled Pauline. "Besides there's loads I can do now I'm here. It may have escaped your notice, but Christmas approaches and I have hardly done or got anything. I don't think I have ever been so ill-prepared."

"I know." A frown crossed his brow. "It's been hard to concentrate on anything lately. We have been through a bad time."

Pauline put her hand on his, instantly wiping away the frown, which had no place in the joyful mood that engulfed them.

"Don't talk about that now," she said gently. "Let's enjoy this moment together and cast everything else out of our minds."

The meal was up to its usual excellent standard. Sipping wine afterwards, with the drink and the mood beginning to weave its mellowing magic, Pauline was unable to resist the question.

"Howard, have you heard the truth about Jason's sudden departure from this world?" There was a mischievous glint in her eye. "Did he really go out with a smile on his face?

Greenfield nodded. "For your ears only, but it seems he did go out in style, yes."

At the invitation of a brief, hastily-typed memo circulated rapidly throughout the building, the entire staff of Impact Publicity Services gathered in the artists' studio, the only room big enough to accommodate so large a crowd, as the seconds ticked away to three-thirty. The half-dozen bottles of champagne, surrounded by packets of paper cups, officially pilfered from vending machine supplies, inspired a constant buzz of expectant chatter.

Dead on the appointed time, Sir Kenneth Craig swept into the room, Howard Greenfield trailing behind him. As the room fell silent, the Chairman of Ibex Holdings made his announcement.

"I am going to be brief, ladies and gentlemen, because I am sure you would rather be sampling the champagne you see here than listening to a long, boring speech from me." A shuffling of feet amongst the audience, most of whom were standing, indicated he was more than likely right. "However, I would like to take a few moments to formally tell you of the board's decision regarding the appointment of a new Managing Director for Impact Publicity Services.

"Firstly, may I say it was with great sadness that I and my colleagues on the board received the news of Jason Henderson's death. He was a loyal and devoted servant of this company, which flourished under his guidance. I am sure all of you, particularly long-serving members of the staff, share equally our sense of loss.

"But we must live in the present and look to the future. The board felt it important a successor should be quickly appointed and saw the ideal candidate within our own ranks. I am pleased to tell you, effective from nine o' clock to-morrow morning, Mr. Howard Greenfield will be Managing Director of Impact Publicity Services."

It was a popular appointment, bringing forth a round of enthusiastic ap-plause, over which could be heard one or two cries of "Well done, Howard!"

When the noisy appreciation tapered off, Sir Kenneth concluded, "Now, ladies and gentlemen, I think we will pop the corks on these bottles and have our own little celebration. I'm sure there is nothing so desperate at this time that it can't wait until tomorrow morning."

Greenfield mingled with his colleagues, readily accepting the plaudits and congratulations. This was his moment, the realisation of a cause to which he had devoted all his working life. He was going to enjoy every second, savour every handshake, every pat on the back.

It was about an hour into the celebrations, the champagne well and truly despatched, that Sandra pushed her way through to him. Because of the din, she had to lift her mouth to his ear to make herself heard.

"I'm sorry, Howard, there's a man on the telephone who insists on speaking to you. He won't give a name. Says you wouldn't recognise it anyway. Claims he must speak to you. Very important, he says."

Greenfield laughed. "Alright Sandra, this afternoon I'll talk to anyone. I'll come and take it on the switchboard."

Following Sandra into the comparative quiet of the reception area, he picked up the switchboard telephone.

"Greenfield here, what can I do for you?"

"A great deal, I think Mr. Greenfield," said the voice into his ear. "Your assignment has been chosen. The time has come for you to fulfil your obligations to us."

Sandra became alarmed as she watched the colour drain from his face. He suddenly seemed unsteady on his feet, so much so that Sandra feared he was going to fall before he desperately steadied himself.

"Are you all right, Howard?" she asked, with obvious concern, but he nodded, making a gesture of reassurance with his free hand. Nevertheless, he had to lean against the switchboard table as his knees weakened once more, threatening to buckle beneath him.

Today, for the first time since falling into the nightmare in Barcelona, he had managed to forget the threat hanging over him. The overwhelming joy of his success had pushed it completely from his mind. It was heading towards three months since those fateful few days. He had even begun to wonder if he dared hope they had forgotten about him or possibly decided they could not use him. Was it really possible these people wanted him to kill someone?

"Are you still there, Mr. Greenfield?" said the voice on the telephone.

"Yes, I'm here," replied Greenfield, his voice faltering noticeably.

"Good. Be on the corner of Arthur Road and Gap Road, in Wimbledon, at six o'clock tonight. You will be picked up and issued with your final instructions. Are you familiar with the meeting place, Mr. Greenfield?"

"I know it, yes."

"That's fine. Please be there on time. Failure to make the rendezvous will be construed as a failure to complete the assignment. And you know what that means, don't you?"

Replacing the receiver, Greenfield muttered under his breath, "Oh God, this cannot be happening to me."

It was spoken so quietly even Sandra was unable to make out what he had said. He stumbled against a desk as he left the reception area, making his way uncertainly down the corridor to his office.

Anxiously, Sandra followed behind him. Having worked alongside him for many years, she was upset and worried at the sudden change she had seen sweep over him.

"Please, Howard, what is it?" she implored. "Was it bad news? Is there anything I can do?"

"It's all right, Sandra." He forced a smile. "The occasion and the champagne, that's all. Just leave me alone for a while."

After she had reluctantly withdrawn, he sat in silence, head in hands. So many times he had wondered how he would act when this moment came, trying to imagine what it would feel like to actually take the life of another human being.

They had made it sound so easy. He had enough intelligence to pick the right moment. There would be nothing to connect him with the victim. All he had to do was run. A "hit-and-run man" they had called him, their despicable idea of a joke. In theory, it sounded fine. But could he pull the trigger?

Today, of all days, had not deserved such an ending. He wanted to cry, but the tears would not come.

Chapter Fifteen

The frost was already settling as he waited in the cold, night air at the corner of Arthur Road and Gap Road. It was a few minutes after six when the sleek, dark-coloured Jaguar saloon pulled into the kerb beside him. The back door was opened, an unspoken invitation for him to get in. Allowing only enough time to drop into the rear seat, the car moved off again. As much as he could see in the dark, the man beside him was young, certainly bespectacled, with a rather large nose.

"Good evening, Mr. Greenfield." The man adopted a business-like tone. It could have been a normal business meeting in the office. "As indicated on the telephone, your assignment has come through. You will probably be glad to know your subject is a male. Men seem to find it so much harder to kill a female. We find such misplaced sentimentality a bit of a bore. Not a problem for you, though, Mr. Greenfield. Here is a photograph of your target. His address is written on the back."

Unable to see the photograph very well in the dark, Greenfield slipped it into the inside pocket of his coat.

"What has this man done to deserve such a fate?"

"That is not for you to know, or me either for that matter," said the man, pushing back the spectacles that had begun to slip down his long nose. "We are being paid solely to eliminate this gentleman. It is not within our brief to probe any deeper into the matter." Picking up an object from the floor in front of him, he added, "Here is your weapon, Mr. Greenfield."

Greenfield shuddered at the touch of the cold steel of the silver-grey automatic pistol pressed into his hand. It was an evil, ugly object, which filled him with a barely controllable urge to shake it from his grasp.

"Here is the magazine," announced the long-nosed man, taking back the gun to demonstrate how the magazine fitted into the butt. "The magazine has fifteen shots, but you shouldn't need anything like that many."

Greenfield let his head fall back against the top of the seat, a gesture of despair.

"This is ridiculous. I've never even handled a gun before in my life. How am I expected to fire one with any degree of accuracy?"

"Simply by getting so close you cannot miss. The gun is specially made to our requirements. It is lightweight, with virtually no recoil. As the subject should have no reason to suspect you, you should be able to get right up close. Fire off a number of shots and you cannot miss." Greenfield slipped the pistol and magazine into a side pocket of his overcoat, as the man continued the instructions. "In addition to your subject's address, you will find on the back of the photograph what we consider may be your best opportunity to carry out the task. You see how helpful we try to be. Whatever you decide, the assignment must be completed by the weekend."

"I don't know if I can do it."

"That is in your hands, of course, but I'm sure you do not need me to remind you of the price of failure. I think you will do it, Mr. Greenfield."

"How can I be sure that will be the end of it?"

"You will have to take our word for it. We are a large international, professional corporation, not a bunch of petty criminals. As such, we operate to a strict code of ethics. If we say that will be the end of it, then so it shall. In any case, we have never used an eliminator more than once. It becomes too risky."

"Will I get the film back? How do I know you haven't made copies of it already?"

"Please, Mr. Greenfield, you really must trust us. When your assignment is completed, you will receive in the post the key to a safety deposit box in a bank somewhere in the London area. Details of the exact location and any necessary documentation to gain access to the box will come under separate cover, for obvious reasons of security. There you will find the film. No copies have been made, nor will there be, if you do what is required of you."

The car crawled to a halt in the kerb at the exact spot from where Greenfield had been picked up, confirming his supposition that they had been driving aimlessly around in circles. Pushing open the car door, the meeting obviously at an end, there was one final question to ask.

"Does this man I am to kill have a name?"

"Names are not very important to us," replied the long-nosed man. "Quite often our subjects do not use their real names anyway. If it is really of interest to you, the name we have for this one is Morgan – Tommy Morgan."

Pauline Greenfield stood at the open bedroom door scarcely able to believe the scene before her.

She had been in the kitchen when she heard her husband come in through the front door. It was a moment she had looked forward to all through the afternoon. The bottle of champagne, the most expensive she could find, purchased while up in the city, was in the ice bucket. This was a great day in their lives; it was a night for celebration. She was desperate not to lose the mood of their lunchtime meeting, build on it, make it strong enough to wipe out the gloom and despair which had threatened to tear their lives apart. Today was the dawning of a new era for them.

Now her hopes lay in ruins as she watched her husband hurriedly and untidily packing a small suitcase lying open on the bed. Fearing something was amiss she had rushed upstairs as soon as she realised he had gone straight up to the bedroom instead of coming to greet her, but she wasn't prepared for this. Taking a deep breath, she was determined to hold back the tears.

"Howard, are you going to tell me what is going on?"

"I have to go away for a few days." He didn't look at her, continuing his packing. "I'll stay in the company flat. Just till the weekend."

"Do I get to know why?"

"There are some things I need to sort out. It will only be for a few days."

"Things such as what, Howard?"

He stood over the half-full suitcase, staring at its unfolded contents. "I can't tell you, Pauline. Things I have to sort out for myself."

"Can't tell me!" Pauline shouted angrily across the room. "Remember me, Howard, I'm your wife. I've been your wife for fifteen years. And you can't tell me!"

"After a pause, he said simply, "No."

"There's someone else, isn't there?"

At last it was out, the great, unvoiced fear that had haunted her since the onset of her husband's strange behaviour. So often she had pushed it to the back of her mind, not wishing to face it as a real possibility. It could no longer be suppressed.

"I thought we would be celebrating tonight, Howard. I've got the champagne on ice downstairs. But it was my turn lunchtime, wasn't it? Tonight you're celebrating with someone else."

"You're not making sense, Pauline."

But the valve had been opened on the fear and anger bottled up inside her for so long, allowing it to gush out as an unstoppable force.

"In the company flat too, how very convenient. Did she go to Spain with you, Howard? Is that the reason for your behaviour since then? Tell me the secret, Howard, what's the attraction? Is she better in bed than I am? Of course, she is probably younger. Knocking off a younger woman seems to be the management trend at Impact these days. Perhaps you should have a doctor check out your heart, see if you can last the pace."

"Pauline, this is nonsense. There isn't anyone else."

"Then tell me why you are going."

"I can't." Greenfield moved towards her, his arms outstretched. "Please try to understand. This is something I have to sort out for myself."

"Don't touch me." The abruptness of her tone shocked him, stopping his move towards her. "If you're going, just go. Clear out. The sooner, the better."

She turned and ran downstairs.

Greenfield finished his packing with a heavy heart. How could a day that had started so marvellously end in such utter desolation? He couldn't tell Pauline the truth. How could he make her believe there was no-one else?

Leaving his suitcase in the hallway, he went into the kitchen where his wife stood, dry-eyed, staring out of the window.

"Please, Pauline, there is no other woman." Choked with emotion, his voice was breaking up. "I have problems in my life right now only I can overcome. No-one can help me. In a few days I'll be back and we can get back to normal. We'll make it a really good Christmas this year."

"Just go, Howard. She'll be wondering where you are."

Greenfield made to continue his pleas, but no words came out. What use was it, anyway?

"Daddy, why don't you love us anymore?"

A thunderbolt could not have dealt him a greater blow. His whole body sagged at his daughter's words. He had not even been aware of her coming into the kitchen behind him.

"I do love you, darling, very much, both you and mummy. Things will be better soon, you'll see."

When he moved forward to kiss her forehead, his daughter turned away, running to her mother's side. He looked at them both in silent agony. There was nothing more he could say.

When the front door had shut behind him, Pauline lifted the chilled bottle of champagne from the ice bucket, before tipping the chunks of ice, with a noisy clatter, into the sink. As hot water from the tap turned them rapidly to liquid and swilled them away, she couldn't help thinking that fifteen years of marriage was going down the drain with them.

Later, in the silent seclusion of the company flat, Howard Greenfield sat staring at the gun in his hand. It was a cold, unfriendly object, as befitted an instrument of death.

Walking over to the full-length mirror on the wall, he lifted up the gun, pointing it straight between the eyes of his own reflection. Could he really do it? They made it seem so easy; pull the trigger and run. For nearly three months he had agonised over what he would do when the time came. Yet, finally, fate had stepped in to tip the scales. If the telephone call had come a week before, or a month before, he would have wrestled for days with the dilemma. On this day it had taken only hours. There really was no choice. He had achieved his ultimate career ambition, an obsession which had dominated years of work, dedication and sacrifice. Nothing was going to cheat him out of that. Flickering memories of the film of he and Julie in Barcelona rattled around his brain. He had no doubt these people would carry out their threat if he failed to carry out this execution. But to take a man's life? The events of the day had ended the dilemma. Now there was too much to lose, much too much.

Squeezing the trigger of the unloaded gun, he said quietly, "You picked a hell of a bloody time to go, Jason."

Chapter Sixteen

Friday dawned bright and sunny, but with a temperature struggling to get above freezing point. Pauline Greenfield was up early, having decided she could not endure another day of inactivity. Her husband had made no contact since leaving on Tuesday evening; neither had she made any attempt to get in touch with him.

Though she would have preferred not to, she decided she must see David Maddocks. She had to find out what it was he had that he felt she should see, so important he couldn't tell her over the telephone. Perhaps he had uncovered the key to the whole tragic mess.

However, that was not her first priority as she went into Diane's bedroom shortly before seven o'clock to ensure her daughter was awake. Sitting on the side of the bed, Pauline said, "Darling, I think we'll forget school today. I am going to take you to Aunt Valerie's for a few days, while your daddy and I sort ourselves out."

"Oh, do I have to?" her daughter moaned sleepily. "I don't mind missing school, but I would rather stay here with you."

"I know you would and I wish you didn't have to go, but I think it's for the best." Putting an arm around Diane's shoulders, Pauline gently kissed the top of her head. "It won't be for long, I promise. Then you'll come back and we'll have a really super Christmas."

She wondered if her lack of conviction showed in her voice. Time ticked away as Diane dithered, as if deliberately trying to delay the moment when she would have to leave, so that Pauline constantly had to hurry her along.

The journey to her sister's took close on two hours, a country drive that Pauline usually enjoyed, yet on this occasion hardly noticed. Reluctant as Diane had been to leave her home, there was no hiding her delight as they entered her Aunt Valerie's house. Her eyes lit up at the decorations covering the walls, bunches of balloons in all sorts of crazy shapes and sizes, the holly flaunting its bright red berries, trying to outdo the lily-white mistletoe. A Christmas tree stood regally in the corner, draped in sparkling silver and gold tinsel.

It was a totally different atmosphere to that which she had unwillingly left a couple of hours before. Here was warmth spawned only by the happiness of a home and the people within it. Pauline was glad to see the transformation in her daughter. It was so easy for people to become so wrapped up in their own problems to a point where they underestimate or ignore the effect it may be having on a son or daughter. "She's only a child, she doesn't really understand." The phrase rolls easily off the tongue. But they do and they hurt.

Expecting a barrage of questions from Valerie, Pauline tried to avoid being alone with her. However, when Valerie announced, with Diane settled doing, under protest, school work in the living room, that coffee had been poured in the kitchen, it became difficult without causing some sort of scene in front of her daughter.

"What's going on?" Valerie asked bluntly, stirring a spoonful of sugar into her coffee, as they sat facing each other across a small, wooden table in the kitchen.

"Still putting sugar in your coffee," Pauline observed evasively, striving to avoid eye contact with her sister. "Give it up. Bad for you and it spoils the taste of the coffee."

Not hiding her impatience, Valerie tried again. "Pauline, are you going to tell me what's going on?"

"Not if I can avoid it, no."

"You can't," Valerie insisted. "You can't take your daughter out of school, make a two-hour drive to bring her to me for a few days while, you're telling me, you and Howard sort some things out and expect not to offer any further explanation than that. This is your sister you're talking to. Now tell me everything."

Pauline sat back in her chair with a deep sigh. This was a conversation she had been desperate not to have, knowing realistically it would be difficult to avoid. She didn't tell Valerie absolutely everything, but gave instead a broad outline of events around Howard's trip to Barcelona, his behaviour since and her suspicions that another woman was involved.

"You don't know for sure there's someone else," offered Valerie, after reflecting for a few moments on what she had heard. "Howard says there isn't. Why should you not believe him?"

"Convince me there's another explanation."

"What are your inner feelings about Howard?" Valerie asked. "Do you love him?"

"For Heaven's sake Val, you tell me what love is," said Pauline, throwing her arms up in exasperation, "and I'll tell you if I love him."

"Love is different things to different people, but you would know it if you felt it."

Despite the sombre tone of the conversation, Pauline couldn't hide a flicker of a smile. "Now you're sounding like something out of Mills and Boon."

Not averse to a slight lightening of the mood, Valerie shared the moment with the briefest of laughs, but insisted, "That doesn't make it any less true."

"I don't know, Val. Until this all blew up, I had come to feel a great closeness to him, a joy of sharing my life with his, thinking of things not just in relation to me, but to both of us. When he's away I miss waking up beside him in the morning and the pleasure of hearing his car pull onto the driveway in the evenings. Now I feel a great emptiness in my life at the possibility of losing all this." Pauline's voice quavered, but she held back the tears. The last thing she wanted to do was cry in front of her sister. "If all that is what love is to me, then I guess I love him."

Valerie reached across the table to take hold of Pauline's hand as she saw her sister's eyes moisten, though no tears fell.

"You told me you didn't love him when you married him," Valerie recalled. "You were honest with me about that."

"That's true," Pauline said, squeezing her sister's hand. "I'm sure it's easier to know what love isn't than what it is. Other guys I'd been in relationships with were nice enough, but no-hopers. Howard was different. I could see where Howard was going and knew he would give me the life-style I wanted. Feelings can change and grow, though, Val. Perhaps it's Diane that's brought us closer together, I don't know. He's been a wonderful father; he's very proud of her and she adores him. It's taken time, but my feelings now are not the same as when I married him. I'm not sure I can face a life with him not being around."

Valerie picked up the coffee mugs, moving to put them on the work surface beside the sink.

"There's no way Howard could have found out about David?" she asked, leaning back against the kitchen unit as she turned to face Pauline.

"Not unless you've told him; you're the only one I have ever told. In any case there's nothing to find out about David. He's just a friend."

"Then why haven't you told Howard about David?"

"Val, you know it doesn't work like that."

"Then just how does it work, Pauline? You're seeing another man, for Christ's sake."

"I'm not seeing another man, as you put it. David's just a friend. It's a platonic relationship, not a romantic one."

"He doesn't see it as platonic."

"I can handle that." Pauline stood up from the table, putting on her coat in readiness to leave. "God knows Val, I wouldn't want to change Howard for the world, but life with him can be so serious and intense sometimes. David is the total opposite. He has a fun attitude to life, sees work as a job, not a career, makes me laugh and he's good to be around for short periods, but it's all pretty shallow. This is why his wife divorced him and he is never going to be competition for Howard."

Pauline went into the living room to say farewell to Diane with what she hoped felt like a reassuring hug and kiss. She wished she really felt the reassurance herself. Back in the hallway, she moved towards the front door, hoping to avoid further conversation with her sister, but Valerie appeared alongside before grabbing her arm and pulling her back into the kitchen.

"First thing you do is get rid of the light relief."

This wasn't something Pauline wanted to talk about, but it seemed her only line of escape.

"I already have," she replied, hoping that would be enough to placate her sister, so she could withdraw from any elaboration. "David's history."

Valerie was having none of it. There was something in the manner and tone of Pauline's announcement of David's demise that indicated there was more to it than a straight forward rejection.

"Why did you not tell me that earlier?" probed Valerie. "What were you hiding? Tell me what happened with David?"

"It was nothing." Pauline awkwardly looked up at the ceiling and around the walls, anywhere but into her sister's eyes. "It was just a kiss."

"Just a kiss," Valerie exploded. "I assume we're not talking a peck on the cheek here. Pauline, whatever were you thinking about?"

"It didn't mean anything," Pauline blustered. "I was stressed out with worry about Howard. I was very vulnerable."

"And David took full advantage. He's been trying to get you into his bed for two years, Pauline; he saw a chink in your armour, went for it and you let him in."

"It was a mad, bad moment, but I pulled away and ended it with David." Pauline put a hand on Valerie's arm. "Don't make me out to be the bad guy in this situation."

"No-one's making you out to be the bad guy," said Valerie, pulling her sister to her and enveloping her in a long, affectionate hug. "I just want things to work out for you and Howard. You have to find him and talk to him. You have to make him open up to you."

"I wish it were that simple," answered Pauline, pulling away from her sister's comforting arms.

"And definitely no more David."

"No more David, I promise."

It was after midday when Pauline eased her Metro on to the car park at Clinton Nuts and Bolts Limited. She looked up at the red-brick office building, full of apprehension. Why was there such a powerful urge to turn the car around, drive away, keep on driving, never knowing the truth? The urge was resisted. She had to know.

Knowing where she was headed, she felt badly about the promise she had made to Valerie, but she had to get out of that house and her sister's probing. She had to see David one more time. The pretty, dark-haired girl at the reception desk welcomed her with a smile.

"Good morning, can I help you?"

"I would like to see Mr. Maddocks, please."

"I'll just see if he is free. What name shall I say?"

"Tell him it's Mrs. Greenfield."

Turning way, the receptionist pushed a button and spoke briefly into the telephone. Returning to Pauline, she said, "He's got someone with him at the moment, but he should be free in about ten minutes. He says he would be delighted to see you if you can spare the time to wait."

Nodding her thanks, Pauline settled in one of a couple of easy chairs set in the carpeted reception area. It would have been better if she had not had to wait. The last thing she needed at the moment was time to think, time to ponder whether she was making a mistake. There was still time to get up and leave.

"Mr. Maddocks will see you now, Mrs. Greenfield, through the double doors, second door on the right."

Pauline's watch told her she had waited nearer fifteen minutes than ten. The office was small, with two wooden desks, set at right-angles to each other, littered with papers and brochures. Plastered around the walls were posters extolling the virtues of an amazing number of nuts and bolts, this thread and that thread, this head and that head. A VDU stood in isolation on its own table, the small green cursor flashing monotonously in the top left hand corner of the otherwise blank screen.

"Pauline, how marvellous to see you." David Maddocks, behind one of the paper-strewn desks, stood up to welcome her, his eyes wandering blatantly down the length of her body. "I'm sorry you had to wait. Have to keep the customers happy."

"Of course," said Pauline, accepting his gestured invitation to take the seat in front of his desk. "I didn't expect to walk straight in without making an appointment."

"Good God, Pauline," beamed David. "You don't have to make an appointment to see me. I'm always delighted to see you, though I would normally prefer it to be in less formal surroundings."

"This is a formal visit, David, not a social one." She was curt and unsmiling. "You said on the telephone you had something I should see."

"Well, yes, that's true." He permitted himself the flicker of a grin at the thought of the envelope in his top, left-hand drawer. "But I think we might discuss it better over a drink, or a spot of lunch, in a more relaxed environment." With a glance at his watch, he added, "If you can hang on just a few minutes longer, I can......"

"Stop playing games, David," interrupted Pauline, her patience pushed to the limit. "I am not going for a drink with you. I am not going to lunch with you. Those days are over, finished with. What do I have to do to make you understand that? Now please, show me what it is I should see."

Deciding to press the lunch invitation no further, David lifted the envelope out of the drawer. It had to come, the moment he had waited for since the report arrived on his desk. For two years he had lived with a consuming desire for this woman. In his hand, he was sure, he held the passport to its fulfilment.

"You said you wanted to know what, if anything, happened to Howard when he was in Barcelona." David paused for effect, hopefully adding to her air of anticipation. "Well, I hired a firm of private investigators in Spain to look into your husband's movements during his stay. What I have here is their report."

"You what!" Pauline's eyes widened, ablaze with amazement and anger. "By what right did you do that? I don't believe this!"

The vehemence of her response startled him. This was not what he expected.

"I was concerned about you," he protested. "I wanted to set your mind at ease, one way or the other."

He could hardly admit to the true reason for his commissioning the investigation.

Her anger remained unabated. "How could you go to such lengths without consulting me first? Who the hell do you think you are, intruding into our private lives to this extent? How dare you check on my husband's movements without seeking my permission? I can't believe your arrogance. Do you really think I would have gone along with such an exercise?"

The awareness of the irony in her vociferous defence of the man she was sure was cheating on her did nothing to quell her rage. She did want to know if there was another woman in Howard's life, but she would never have gone to such lengths. The thought of some seedy private eye in far off places probing into her husband's activities filled her with revulsion.

"I'm sorry, I thought I was doing the right thing." For David it had all gone wrong. He sat bemused and deflated. This was not the reaction he had expected from Pauline. There was meant to be anger, plenty of it, but not directed at him; directed instead at Howard after she had read the report. He had been ready to fan the flames of this anger into a fiery crescendo that would finally burn itself out in his bed. Now it looked as if she wasn't even going to read the report. "And, don't forget, it was you who brought me into your problems in the first place."

"I just wanted someone to talk to about them, that's all."

"What can I say?" he said weakly, spreading his arms in a gesture of helplessness.

"Nothing." Pauline violently pushed back the chair as she stood up. "I don't think there is anything more for us to say to each other at all. Don't try to get in touch, David. Stay out of my life – for good!"

"Pauline," he called after her a she made for the door, but the fire in her eyes told him further protest was useless. Instead he picked up the envelope and held it towards her. "You might as well take this anyway."

Staring at the envelope, she began to tremble. Her every instinct told her she shouldn't take it. Wasn't she so enraged that it existed at all? She should have the courage of her convictions, tell him to throw it in the garbage where it belonged. The envelope hung tantalisingly in front of her, daring her to turn away without learning the secrets of its contents. Did it really have the answer?

She snatched it from his hand. "This doesn't make it right, David."

As she disappeared through the door, David kicked the side of his desk in frustration. He had played his trump card and still lost – for ever, it seemed.

Pauline sat in her car in the car park outside the offices for five minutes looking at the envelope lying on top of the dashboard, trying to find the courage to open it. It was too real. Here were not worries, suspicions or suppositions; this was fact. She still had a tiny lifeline of hope to cling to, a possibility, however remote, that she was wrong about Howard. The contents of that envelope could break that lifeline in two.

The hand she finally forced to reach out shook visibly. Neatly typewritten, under the heading of an unpronounceable name, though it was possible to decipher the address was somewhere in Madrid, the report, despite its brevity, made harrowing reading:

"Mr. Howard Greenfield, hereinafter referred to as the subject, stopped at the Hotel Husa Presidente, Barcelona, on the nights of September 20th/21st this year. On the first night, at approximately 8.40 p.m. local time, he was met in the foyer of the hotel by a woman. The woman was said to be in her twenties, height around 160 cm (5 feet 3 inches), blonde, very attractive with particularly striking eyes. Their meeting appeared to be a social one and they left immediately in a taxi. The couple went to a restaurant where they dined, leaving together shortly before 11.00 p.m. local time. The subject was observed to return to the hotel shortly after 4 a.m. local time the following morning. A few hours later, at 9.30 a.m. local time, the subject was met again by this woman and they left the hotel together once more."

There followed an uninteresting list of business appointments. Pauline would have liked to see more detail; what happened after they left the restaurant, where did they go? She considered the report not a particularly efficient piece of work, but had no way of knowing the level of competence had been regulated by the automatic pointed at the investigator's forehead. Yet what it did say was damning enough.

A letter accompanying the report stated. "As we have been unable to establish the identity of this woman and think now we have little chance of doing so, we feel there is no justification in continuing this investigation at your expense with so little hope of it being productive."

Pauline could no longer hold back the tears. Letting her head fall onto the rim of the steering wheel, she sobbed uncontrollably. Overhead the winter sun had given way to dark swirling clouds. The first signs of an icy drizzle sprinkled across the windscreen.

Chapter Seventeen

Howard Greenfield parked his car in the car park of the Mole with Two Heads with drinking the last thing on his mind. According to the information on the back of the photograph, this was where Tommy Morgan would be that night. The A-Z road map showed only one logical route back to his apartment in Milverton Road, leaving Greenfield only to pick the right spot to carry out his task.

Pulling his overcoat collar up around his ears, protection against the biting wind and freezing drizzle, he set off along Hopdale Avenue. The terraced houses, fronted by tiny gardens, running the whole length of both sides, were not what he was hoping for. When School Road seemed to be offering only more of the same, he was unable to contain a growing sense of foreboding. Houses meant people. The first few minutes after he had carried out the kill were vital to him. Every second that elapsed before anybody realised what had happened or reached the scene was a second longer to run, another step between him and the body he would have left sprawled on the pavement.

He was getting towards the crossroads over which stood Milverton Road itself, when the scenery suddenly changed. The houses suddenly ended, giving way to a playground and the school that obviously gave the road its name. Across the street, behind high green railings, were the school's playing fields, with, so far as he could see, one muddy soccer pitch and an equally soggy hockey pitch. Along the final hundred yards or so of School Road there were no houses.

The street lighting looked to be poor, old-fashioned, with lampposts too far apart to give adequate illumination. The crossroads provided an escape route.

It looked right. This was where it would happen. This was where he would kill Tommy Morgan.

Greenfield couldn't explain the compulsion that took him in to Milverton Road. Having accomplished what he had set out to do, there was no need to go on, yet he continued walking, into the road where Tommy Morgan lived.

The houses were different here, much larger and mostly detached, probably once the homes of the reasonably well off he suspected. Now they were rotting away with neglect, divided up into apartments.

Greenfield stopped in front of number fifteen, looking up at the paint flaking off the crumbling woodwork surrounding the large window on the first floor. He wondered if Morgan was in there now, this close to him. What was he doing this very moment? There was no sign that Morgan was up there, this man who looked so young and full of life on the photograph. Perhaps he went to work, not much of a way to spend the last day of one's life. It was difficult to imagine what he could have done to bring such a fate down on himself. Why would someone want him dead?

"Can I help you?"

Greenfield was startled by the voice breaking into his thoughts. Wheeling round, the words he began to utter in reply stuck in his throat. He was looking straight into the face on the photograph. This was something he had not wanted to happen. Not this closely. He cursed himself for not turning back at the school, sparing himself the torture of looking into those bright, brown eyes he was soon to close for ever.

Morgan spoke again. "Are you all right, my friend?"

Greenfield struggled to regain his composure. This was a bad mistake, but all he could do now was extricate himself from it as best as he could.

"Er, yes, of course," he stammered. "You, er, gave me a bit of a start, that's all. I was miles away."

"I'm sorry." Did Morgan have to smile that way? Why couldn't he be hostile and abusive? "Are you sure I can't be of any help?"

"I'm looking for a flat. I wondered if there were any vacancies around here." Greenfield had to say something. That was all he could think off.

Morgan looked him up and down, taking in the smart, obviously expensive clothes. "If you don't mind me saying so, I would have thought you could do better for yourself than Milverton Road."

Greenfield searched for a plausible reply. "It's only for a couple of days a week when I am up in town, so I wouldn't want anything very expensive."

"Well, these are probably as cheap as you will find in London," agreed Morgan, "but you have got to live with the fungus decorating the walls and get friendly with the lice trotting in and out of the woodwork. I am not sure that would be your style."

Greenfield forced a smile. "Perhaps not."

Moving past him, Morgan said, "Still, if you are really interested and can wait a few days, my flat should be vacant next week. I'm going home."

Home? Where was home? Greenfield had not thought any further than this run-down apartment. Was there a wife waiting somewhere for this man, children perhaps? Greenfield wondered how much grief he would cause that night when he snuffed out this young life prematurely.

"Can I help you, can I help you?" These first few words Morgan had spoken reverberated round his brain as he made his way back to the car, hammer blows making an indelible imprint on his mind. Oblivious to his surroundings, he could not get the face out of his mind. He doubted he ever would.

Chapter Eighteen

The vodka bottle was empty. Lifting her glass, Pauline swallowed the last dregs with a gulp, wincing as the burning liquid sprayed the back of her throat. The empty bottle slipped from her hand onto the carpet with a dull thud as she lay back on the settee, all track of time lost, aware only that day had turned to night as the vodka bottle had gone from full to empty. On the floor lay a crumpled piece of paper, a few words typed by a complete stranger in a foreign land that had left her life in ruins.

Far from drowning her sorrows, the alcohol had served only to multiply the tears and cultivate the bitter sense of rejection. Suddenly she was second best, cast on the scrapheap to make way for another woman. What did this blonde with the striking eyes have to offer Howard that she couldn't? Was she really so much more desirable? Pauline had tried to keep herself trim as the years advanced, careful about what she ate, doing a bit of exercise whenever she had the chance. She knew she looked younger than her age, but Howard, it seemed, was expecting too much. She couldn't stop the clock completely.

Lying back in the darkness, she looked in vain for sleep to rescue her from her torment. Fired by the drink, her brain refused to rest. It was she her husband should be making to feel beautiful and wanted, she her husband should be making to feel needed and desirable, not this young blonde-haired pretender to the crown she had held and served loyally for fifteen years.

She sat upright with a jolt.

"Damn you, Howard Greenfield, damn you!" she screamed, hurling her glass across the room, so that it smashed noisily into pieces as it crashed against a wall.

Resting her head on her knees, her whole body shaking as she sobbed loudly, the image burst once more into her mind, a recurring vision that grew vividly stronger with the increasing grip the alcohol was taking on her brain. She seemed powerless to stop it exploding in her head and unable to make it go away when it did.

A man and a woman naked on a bed, their long and searching kisses leaving them gasping for breath, locked in each other's arms so tightly they could have been imagining they would fall off the world if they let go. The face of the woman was an indistinguishable blur except for two features. Pauline could see clearly the blonde hair and a pair of large, seductive eyes. The man's face was not visible to start with, but when he turned over, eagerly pulling the blonde, female image underneath him, there was no mistaking Howard, the husband who had shared her bed for so many years. Pauline put her hands over her eyes, trying to shut out the vision, but she could only watch helplessly as her husband and the woman devoured each other's bodies with their unrelenting passion.

Pauline let out a loud, demented scream. How long must this torture go on?

But it came again, the two naked figures, as though the film had been wound back and restarted. She didn't notice the change at first. It was a gradual realisation that this time the blonde hair and the large eyes had disappeared. Complete and in focus, the woman's face was frighteningly recognisable. Pauline shook her head vigorously. Perhaps she could shake the manifestation from her mind. But it persisted. And there could be no mistake. She was looking at herself.

What was happening now? What was this madness? Even without a view of his face, Pauline could see the man she was pulling hungrily down on top of her was not Howard. The body of this man was bigger, broader. He appeared younger. This vision filled her mind so vividly it seemed real, actually taking place in front of her. She felt she could reach out and touch her own image. Then she saw the man's face. It was David. Desperately she fumbled with the switch of the table lamp beside the settee until light flooded the room, banishing the darkness and wiping the picture from her mind in the same instant.

Pauline lay back exhausted and very drunk. She and David; she could make it happen. An immense sense of satisfaction welled up inside her at the thought that she had no lesser power than the blonde, big-eyed bitch who had lured her husband from her bed. She smiled. David adored her, worshipped her. It was impossible for him to hide it. She could have David any time she chose.

Suddenly her alcohol-ravaged senses were swept by an overwhelming need to see the longing in his eyes that had given her so much secret pleasure. She yearned to feel wanted, to know once more the thrill of exciting a man. She didn't seem to excite her husband any longer. Somebody else excited him now. She needed reassurance that she still had the power.

Struggling to her feet, she had to hold on to the arm of the settee as her unsteady legs threatened to dump her back among the cushions. After a few deep breaths, she managed to make her way slowly to the shower. The warm water dampened some of the drunken fever ravaging her brain, but not enough to weaken her resolve. This was something she had to do. There was no turning back.

She chose a plain, white dress that Howard had always liked because it fitted her tightly, but smoothly, tapering down to just below knee-length with the slightest of slits at the side. Her hair washed and blow-dried, she applied her make-up with meticulous care. She meant to look her best.

Aware that she was in no condition to drive herself, she ordered a taxi on the telephone. Never having been to David's flat before anyway, she wasn't exactly sure how to get there, so would be happy to rely on the taxi driver's superior knowledge of the area.

It would be there in ten minutes the voice on the telephone had said. She took a final look in the tall mirror, first front-ways and the sideways on. Her stomach was not quite as flat these days as she would have liked, but otherwise she was more than happy with what she saw. For a reject, she thought she looked pretty damn good.

Chapter Nineteen

Tommy Morgan was angry. The Beard had returned to the table in the lounge bar of the Mole with Two Heads after taking a telephone call with news that pushed the Irishman close to the limits of his self-control.

Across the room Howard Greenfield tried, through the smoke and dimmed lighting, to make out what was going on. Unfortunately, because of his earlier encounter, he had to sit as far away as possible. The last thing he needed was a wave and a smile from the man he was about to murder. He could see that Morgan had become very agitated, but there was no chance over the noisy buzz of conversation in the crowded room, the over-loud piped music and the incessant chiming of the gaming machines of picking up any trace of what was being said.

In fact, the Beard was trying desperately to calm Morgan down, without much success. "For God's sake, don't make a scene of it," he pleaded, with a restraining gesture of his hands.

"What do you bloody well expect?" Morgan was too fired with rage to be influenced by the pleas for calm. "You said he would definitely be here tonight. I've had my fill of being messed about by you people."

He saw Horace and Lenny tense and wondered how many guns were trained on him under the table.

"I don't know why he has changed his mind," insisted the Beard.

"Didn't he give any indication?"

"Men like him don't give reasons for what they do."

"Well, he'll give reasons to me," Morgan exploded, prompting more gestures for calm from the Beard. "I demand to know what's going on here. I want to know if our deal is still on and, if not, you had better bloody well say so and be done with it. I want to know by tomorrow."

"Who the hell do you think you are with your demands?" spat out the Beard. "Have you any idea who you are dealing with here?"

"Remember for once who *you* are dealing with," seethed Morgan. "You may not care much for our organisation, but you ignore us at your peril. By tomorrow, I said."

"I'll see your message is reported back, but I cannot give you any guarantees. We are not in the habit of responding to threats."

"Then you see four million pounds' worth of heroin go out of the window, because I'm on tomorrow night's boat train. Christmas is only a week or so away and I am a very weary man. I'm going home, deal or no deal."

"For Christ's sake keep your voice down." The Beard's concern was unfounded, for it was impossible to be overheard in the general noise of the crowded room. "Your superiors won't be happy if you go back without a deal."

"When I tell them what's gone down over here, they will probably want to know why I didn't come home earlier. I have been as patient as I can be, taken as much punishment as I am prepared to take. God knows, I've been beaten and abused to the point of death itself, but no more. I'm not going to allow myself or my organisation to be humiliated any further." Morgan finished off the beer in his pint glass. "We'll find another market. Try another country – the States possibly. Probably there's more opportunity out there anyway. Perhaps it's too big for your lot. No belly for it; I believe that was a phrase you once used."

"That's rubbish. There's no question of it being too big for us. I don't know why the boss has cancelled tonight. He wanted to do business with you and I have no reason to believe that has changed."

Morgan got to his feet, leaning forward, his hands on the table. "Then he will have to come to me. There'll be no more meetings here. And make sure it's by tomorrow night, because that's when I'm leaving. Whether the powder goes with me or not is up to you."

Horace and Lenny threw enquiring glances at the Beard, silently asking if they should stop the Irishman from leaving. The Beard shook his head. There was nothing more to be said at this time. Yet the events of the evening did leave him puzzled. He did not know a contract had been put out on Tommy Morgan's life.

Greenfield planned to wait a whole minute after the obviously angry man had left, mentally counting up the seconds. There was no need to hurry. Morgan could only go one way home. Greenfield must not arouse any suspicion that he was deliberately following. It amazed him that he could even think like this. Was it so easy to develop a criminal mind?

On the count of sixty, he left the warmth of the public house and stepped out into the bitterly cold night.

David Maddocks could scarcely believe his eyes. When Pauline had stormed out of his office that morning, he had truly believed he would not see her again. The thought had hung over him all day, swamping him in a cloud of despondency greater than any unhappiness he had ever known before. However infrequent their meetings had been, there was always the next one to look forward to. With her leaving she had taken away a vital part of his life, leaving a void that could never be filled.

Now here she was, standing before him. In no mood for visitors, particularly at such a late hour, he had cursed loudly at the chimes of the doorbell, but the gloom was swept aside by a surging tide of elation at the sight of her.

"Are you going to leave me standing out here all night, David?" she asked with a smile

He suddenly realised he had been standing there for several seconds in a speechless state of shock, simply looking at her.

"Of course not, come in, please. It's just a bit of a surprise, that's all. No, that's an understatement. It's a hell of a surprise. I thought you had walked out of my life for ever this morning."

She slipped slowly past him into the flat, looking up into his eyes as she did so. "This morning was a million years ago."

As David slipped the coat off her shoulders, she turned to face him, looking up into his eyes in eager search of a sign of the impact she intended her appearance, complemented by her chosen figure-hugging dress, to have. She knew she looked good and was not disappointed, certain his eyes visibly widened as they unashamedly ran down her body. Subtlety was not David's strong point, but subtlety was not what she was looking for. She wondered if Howard's blonde whore managed such an effect on him.

Throwing her coat over the back of a chair, David said, "I would still like to say that anything I did was purely out of concern for your welfare. I was very worried about you."

"Leave out the crap, David," she protested. "For two years I have watched the lust in your eyes. I've fed my ego on it. So I know exactly what your intentions were when you hired your Spanish private eye."

"Yet you still came here tonight."

"Yes I still came."

David ran a finger gently down the side of her face. It could be nothing else but a declaration of intent. The defences were breached. The chase was over. In the end the chase had come to him. There is always something special about the moment of awareness that something wonderful is going to take place, something wanted so much for so long. The joy of anticipation is often as sweet as the realisation.

Kicking off her shoes, Pauline draped herself across the sofa, lying back so that her body pressed against the tight-fitting dress as it shifted up above her knees. She wanted to play games and David was content to play along. Settling in an armchair, he resolved to enjoy the preamble. Two years he had waited for this moment, so a few minutes more were easily tolerable in the knowledge that time was all that stood between him and the final surrender of Pauline's body. He had long resigned himself to the fact that only a miracle could save his passion from being forever unrequited. Now that miracle was unfolding around him, he was happy to let it run its natural course.

Pauline giggled. "Tell me, David, do you have erotic fantasies about me?"

He was taken aback by her directness. It was so different to the Pauline he knew, or thought he knew.

"Very often," he answered, "usually at the most embarrassing times. Sometimes at work even, when I'm in a meeting with my boss and suddenly find I haven't heard a word he has said."

"Whatever do you do then?"

"Bend forward, cross my legs, try to look intelligent and hope he hasn't noticed."

Pauline laughed loudly. "I don't believe a word, but I like it. I had erotic fantasies about you this afternoon. Does that shock you?"

"To the core, but don't let that stop you having them."

Curtailing her laughter, Pauline looked around.

"Have you got a drink in this place?"

Sure, there's a tray over there behind you on the sideboard." David stood up. "What would you like?"

"Whisky, vodka, whatever's going."

Bottles of whisky and vodka were included in the selection on the tray, but David preferred the former. As he began to fill two glasses, she came beside him, brushing her arm against his." He felt the knot in his stomach as his body responded to the sensation of her closeness.

"Do I have striking eyes, David?"

"You have very beautiful eyes."

"Presumably that means 'no'." Pauline looked up at him. "What is my best feature then? How would I be described in a private detective's report?"

"Pauline, there's no need to torture yourself this way."

The contradiction was not lost on David even as he spoke the words. The torment Pauline was suffering was exactly what he had set out to create and it had achieved its objective, undoubtedly being the basis of the reasoning that had brought her to him tonight.

"To pick out your outstanding features would mean listing everything about you. You're the most beautiful woman I have ever known or seen in my life. That's not just it though, there's more than that to you, an extra-special something simmering just below the surface; a warm sensuality radiating from you so that just to be in your presence fills me with a joy no other woman has ever aroused in me. If Howard no longer wants to feel that joy, the he's one hell of a bloody fool."

Who made the first move David could never remember, but suddenly she was in his arms, pressing her body against him, her open mouth locked on his, her tongue sliding teasingly across the tip of his. He held her to him as though his very existence depended on her clinging to him, his senses reeling at the urgency of her kisses, his hands running wildly over the body that was soon to be his. No longer was it a dream, no longer a fantasy.

Pulling herself away, Pauline picked up her glass and swallowed a large mouthful of whisky. The alcohol went straight to her head, inducing an intoxication she found highly pleasurable. For two years she had been content to see and be aware of this man's craving for her body. It was no longer enough. Now she needed to know the reality of it. To hell with Howard and his big-eyed blonde.

"You have a nice place here, David, I'm very impressed," she said moving across the room, glass in hand. Pushing open a door with her foot, she added. "This, I presume, is the bedroom."

"You found it in one."

Smiling, she said, "Why don't you join me? You know I hate to drink alone."

Chapter Twenty

The icy drizzle had turned to snow, large, furry flakes swirling around on the freezing wind. They settled in Greenfield's hair as he closed quickly on the figure ahead of him. No more than eight yards between them now, but it was still too much. The awesome awareness of the power in his hands was overwhelming. In that instant, he was God. He held the power of life or death over the man foraging through the snow ahead of him. Such thoughts could not be allowed to thwart his purpose. To preserve Greenfield's life a man must die. That was the way of it.

He was close enough now, only a few feet. Without altering his pace, he pulled the pistol clear of his pocket, held it out in front of him and fired four times, so rapidly the reports sounded almost as one. Even in the poor light he could see the flesh ripped apart as the bullets slammed into the back of Tommy Morgan's head, pitching him forward face-down onto the snow-carpeted pavement.

Greenfield was amazed at the thrill that rushed through his body as he squeezed the trigger. There were no feelings of horror, no revulsion, only a soaring exhilaration at the manifestation of the ultimate power of life or death over another human being. It must have been over in a second or two, yet to Greenfield it seemed an age, the bullet-ridden body arcing away from him in an unreal, dream-like, slow-motion plunge.

It really had been easy, just as they had said it would. He knew the feelings of horror and revulsion would come, but for now the nightmare was over. He had won his freedom. Tomorrow he would be back home, with Pauline and his daughter, Diane, their troubles behind them, the start of a new life. All he had to do now was run.

"Police! Armed Police!" The voice came from behind him. "Stay where you are!"

It couldn't be possible. He was sure he and Morgan had been alone on the street. How could it be the police? He must be dreaming, his imagination playing wild tricks on him. This was the adrenalin rush fevering his brain. No, he had to run. That was all he had to do.

"I repeat, this is the police and we are armed." The voice came again out of the darkness, only closer and louder this time. "Put down your weapon and raise your hands behind your head."

Greenfield's brain was spinning, the inside of his head a swirling whirlpool of confusion. He could see nothing through the darkness and the thickening snowfall. The police couldn't be there. It was impossible. He had to get home to Pauline. He was suddenly filled with an overwhelming longing to be with her, feel the nearness of her, to hold her soft, warm hand in his. How much he needed her now.

His self-control crumbled. Acting on instincts born of fear and panic, he raised the pistol once more, firing wildly in the direction from which the voice came, squeezing the trigger repeatedly, bullet following rapidly upon bullet.

A volley of revolver fire rattled back out of the darkness. Strangely, there was no pain as the bullets smacked into Greenfield's chest, only a sensation of being dealt a rapid series of hefty blows, which sent him staggering back several paces. Desperately he tried to stay on his feet. He had to run, get away from this place. But his strength poured out of him like water gushing from a tap, his legs gave way and he dropped first to his knees before keeling over the snow-covered pavement.

Two men appeared, shadowy forms in the night. One knelt beside Greenfield as he lay on his back gasping for breath. The other went to the man lying just a few feet away. Only the briefest of looks was necessary, no more than the open, unseeing eyes, though that didn't stop a frantic search for any trace of a pulse. With a shake of the head, the man said in despair, "Please tell me this is not happening. Mike's dead. Jesus Christ, the bastards have killed him."

Mike? Who was Mike? Greenfield knew nothing of anyone called Mike.

"This one's still alive. Get on the radio, let's get some help out here."

"I've got a better idea. Step aside and let me put a bullet in his head. That's all the help this low-life scum should get."

The officer kneeling beside Greenfield stood up to face his colleague. The snow was getting heavier, the biting wind colder.

"That's crazy talk. Step back and think about what you are saying. I can understand your rage and anger, God knows I feel it too. Mike was a friend as well as a fellow officer, but we're not executioners. That brings us down to their level. And we need answers to what's gone down here tonight. We need this guy alive."

Greenfield began to shiver. It was so cold. Every breath was becoming more of a struggle, a battle against the great weight seemingly bearing down on his chest, crushing his lungs. The overcoat draped over his body by one of the men failed to stop the shivering.

"What made you do this?" The voice seemed a long way off, barely audible. "Who are you working for?"

If he could have mustered the strength to speak, he could not have answered the questions. He knew nothing. That was how they operated.

Greenfield only just made out the words, "Ambulances are on the way." He was becoming remote from the activity around him, drifting away, the street and the two men fading gently into the distance.

Someone touched his shoulder. "You hold in there. Help is not far away. Don't you dare die on us"

But he was losing the fight. Swirling snow danced contemptuously across his face and settled on the coat covering him as he breathed in desperate gulps, frantically trying to inflate lungs that were losing the struggle to function. It couldn't end like this. This wasn't how it was supposed to happen. He had done the deed, earned his freedom. Now he had to get home to Pauline.

A sudden stab of pain deep in his chest was so vicious it forced him to cry out. And as Howard Greenfield rolled over to die in a cold, snow-swept gutter, his wife was making love with a ferocity she had never known in fifteen years of married life.

Chapter Twenty-One

"It's a bad business."

Sitting in his office in New Scotland Yard, Commander James Hawkes shook his head gravely as he delivered what appeared to be a masterpiece of under-statement to Detective Chief Inspector Richard Proffitt, who slumped wearily in a chair facing him.

"Yes, you never quite get used to losing one of your own, do you?"

"Have you seen his wife?"

"Yes, I broke the news to her." Proffitt rubbed his eyes, already reddened by lack of sleep. "Not a very pleasant duty, but someone had to do it."

"I sympathise. Telling someone of the death of someone close to them is something I've never really got used to. I don't think many of us do. Even more so when it involves people we know personally."

"It goes with the job, I suppose."

"How did she take it?"

"Very badly, as you'd expect. Cried a lot. I left a WPC with her." Proffitt cleared his throat, but was unable to remove the emotional quiver from his voice. "There's a child also, a son, two years old. Slept right through all the commotion, never as much as stirred. God knows what his mother is going to tell him when he wakes up. How do you tell a two-year-old boy, a few days before Christmas, that his father isn't coming home any more?"

"What in blazes went wrong out there, Dick?"

Proffitt sighed heavily. "It doesn't make any sense. Mike Donovan was one of our best under-cover officers. This assignment was tailor-made for him. He had an Irish father, spent most of his childhood over there. He still spoke with a slight accent even. We created an existence out there in Ireland we were sure would stand up to any enquiries that they made. Everything was covered, we were sure of it."

"That doesn't seem to have been the case."

"They must have found a chink in the armour somewhere." Proffitt wasn't sure which he wanted more, a double whisky or simply to close his eyes and sleep. "Heaven knows how or what. Perhaps sometimes we underestimate the intelligence of the criminal classes."

"We shouldn't."

"I know, but I think we do."

Commander Hawkes leaned forward on his desk, looking Proffitt straight in the eye and asked, "There's no chance of a leak from inside, is there? Someone on a payroll other than our own? How many officers knew about this operation?"

Proffitt didn't react to the Commander's stare, but was knocked back by the question.

"Counting you and me, no more than six," Proffitt replied, "but I would trust my life with any of them, including your good self."

Proffitt had known James Hawkes throughout his police career, having served with him in the early days in uniform on the streets. Hawkes had never come over to him as a particularly outstanding officer or a particularly ambitious one, so continued to view the rise to his current position with some surprise. He wondered why he, with two commendations for bravery, one for rescuing two young children from a blazing building and more recently for grappling with and disarming an escapee from a mental institution running amok on Oxford Street with a Samurai sword, seriously injuring a number of lunch-time shoppers, seemed to have hit the buffers at Detective Inspector. Perhaps, he wondered, you just might be too useful out on the street to be promoted to a chair behind a desk.

Commander Hawkes leaned back in his chair.

"There's going to be a major inquiry into this whole affair and every option will be examined, including the possibility of someone on the inside giving Donovan up."

"Given the circumstances," Proffitt conceded, "I would expect nothing less."

Hawkes was not looking forward to the scrutiny this disastrous mess would bring down on him. He was looking to move further up the career ladder and this would not look good on his CV. How he wished it was all a bad dream, from which he would soon awaken. He shifted uncomfortably in his chair, a big man, over six feet tall with middle-age catching up on his body, his face growing more rounded, his hair greying and he was sure when he looked in the mirror that morning there were signs of bags appearing beneath his eyes. Pulling nervously at his white shirt collar, he began to feel very warm in his uniform and wasn't sure it was entirely due to the overworked room heating.

"Tell me, why were two officers following Donovan? Did you order that?"

Proffitt shook his head. "Call it a copper's gut instinct. It was just a feeling Peters and Tanner had that something wasn't quite right. There was no reason to think that. I had terminated the night's proceedings. Theoretically they were off duty."

"Didn't their instincts tell them to stop this fellow...er... Greenfield?" Hawkes had to consult a piece of paper lying on his desk to be sure of the name. "Could they not have done something to prevent this thing happening?"

"The last thing Peters and Tanner were expecting was someone walking brazenly up to Donovan on the street and blasting four bullets into his body," said Proffitt. "Don't forget they had no reason to suspect anything was going to happen at all. They also had to keep a discreet distance for fear of blowing his cover. This was still very much an on-going operation. Then it all happened so quickly. This man Greenfield closed up, produced a gun and it was over in a matter of seconds. It doesn't make a lot of sense. It's certainly not the way you would expect a pro. to operate. And yet, if Peters and Tanner hadn't been there, he would probably have got away with it. He picked a spot away from the houses, could have been away before anybody realised what had happened. A respectable business executive, no criminal record, no known criminal contacts or associates, there would have been absolutely nothing to connect him with the murder of an undercover policeman."

"Couldn't Peters and Tanner have stopped and searched him with a bit of tact and discretion?"

"Discreetly or otherwise, on what grounds?" Proffitt opened his hands in a gesture of helplessness. "It was only around a quarter to ten last night, hardly a time when a mere presence on the street could be viewed with suspicion and these officers were armed, remember. If the guy had turned out to be as innocent as he looked, there would have been hell to pay. The media and some of our politicians would have had a field day, questions in the House probably.

"I'm sure they will, anyway. The headlines will make it sound like a Wild West shoot-out on the streets of London. I have a press conference to chair in a few minutes and you know how I hate doing those."

"We walk a thin political tightrope sometimes. It's a fact of life. But there was much more to this one. Our chaps had no way of knowing Donovan was under some sort of surveillance or that his life was in any immediate danger. We had no way of knowing for certain how much the people he was dealing with trusted him. No, Peters and Tanner had to be one hundred per cent sure Donovan was at risk before they acted, otherwise they could have blown the whole operation or even exposed Donovan to the very danger they were seeking to protect him from."

"And by the time they were certain, it was all over, I suppose."

In the bad weather conditions and the dark I doubt they even saw the gun. Probably the first they knew was when the shots were actually fired."

"What about the pub earlier, what went on there?"

"We have been after this drugs syndicate for months now. We know they are big, but they are also well organised. Our enquiries were getting nowhere. Donovan went under cover with remarkable success. He had a meet set up with their number one, their top man. We were that close. For some reason the man never showed. Donovan put on an impressive show of anger and left."

"Who did show up?"

"Some freelance muscle, Lenny Carson and Horace Pemberton, all brawn, no brains, do their bit for anyone prepared to pay. What was interesting was Miles Brassington, usually calls himself the Beard, for obvious reasons. A nasty piece of work this one, even more so because he has the brains to go with it. University graduate, got his degree with honours. Could have had a brilliant career in the civil engineering line. We have a thick file on Mr Brassington, but, incredibly, he has no form to date. Plenty of suspicion, but he's simply been too clever for us. We've never been able to prove a thing. What was worrying about his showing up at the meet is that we think he may have Mafia connections. I said we knew this syndicate was big, but it could be it's much bigger than we thought."

"If we had a file on Brassington, wouldn't Donovan have known him?"

"Possibly, But I doubt it. There's no way of knowing for sure. Donovan filed no regular reports on this one and we didn't keep him under surveillance until last night when we thought the top dog was putting in an appearance. We thought it was too risky. We only had two telephone calls, both from public call boxes, only long enough to pass on bare essentials; one to tell us he had made contact initially, the other yesterday to tell us of last night's meet. Otherwise, we had no contact with him. He was set up with his new identity in his own place before he started putting the feelers out and for the past month he lived that identity totally and utterly."

"Are you saying his wife hadn't seen him for the past month?" Commander Hawkes eyes widened, his bushy eyebrows raised. Proffitt nodded. "My God, the poor woman."

Proffitt said quietly, "Yes."

The two men fell silent, struck by the enormity of the impact last night's news must have had on Mike Donovan's wife in such circumstances. After a pause long enough for Proffitt to presume the interview was over, so that he was about to dismiss himself, Commander Hawkes continued, "What do you know about this Greenfield fellow?"

"Very little so far, certainly nothing as yet to give any indication why he did what he did. Howard Greenfield seems to have been a highly respectable and respected business executive at the height of his career, promoted only this week to Managing Director of the advertising agency he worked for. He certainly found a strange way to celebrate his success."

"Have you spoken to his wife?"

"Yes, but only within the last hour. She wasn't at home last night. She broke down completely at the news, so much so we had to get a doctor to her. He put her under sedation, so we haven't really got anything at all from her yet."

"That's a pity; we could do with talking to her. There is always a possibility Greenfield had a personal motive. We are presuming Donovan's murder was something to do with his undercover operation, but that may not be necessarily so."

Proffitt nodded his agreement. "I had considered the personal angle, but somehow it doesn't seem very likely to me. Mike Donovan wasn't the sort to make enemies outside his police work. He liked the quiet life, devoted to his wife and kid. Although it's too early at this stage to be sure of anything, nothing has turned up so far to show any previous link between Donovan and Greenfield. My guess is they never even met before last night. No, I think we must presume at the moment Donovan was killed because of his undercover activities. How or why Howard Greenfield became the man to do it is a mystery that may never be solved. The answer could well have gone to the grave with him."

"No leads from the gun?"

"Forensics is checking it now, but I don't think they are going to find anything that will help us much. Automatic pistol, seemed to be custom-built, no manufacturer's name, no identifying marks of any sort. This is what gives this killing a professional touch, yet I can't see Howard Greenfield, advertising executive, as having a secret career as a hired gun. I think we face an uphill struggle on this one. There are too many unanswered questions only Greenfield himself could give us the answers to."

"Keep me informed of any progress, however small." Commander Hawkes gathered together the papers on the desk before him, indicating that now the meeting really was at a close. "Losing one of our own officers in the line of duty is always a bitter pill to swallow, Dick. Like losing a member of your own family. It also knocks morale for six, brings out all the suppressed anxieties, fills the place with an air of gloom that is difficult to shake off. An unsolved mystery to go with it isn't going to help any, so let's have maximum effort on this one."

"We'll give it everything we've got."

Hawkes nodded. "Good. The Commissioner will want your report in writing, of course, but for the moment I'll give him a verbal one based on what you have told me."

"I.P.C.C. will be involved I assume."

"Ah, the Independent Police Complaints Commission," Commander Hawkes sighed, adding sarcastically, "what would be do without them? Yes, I had to refer it and they've already been on the telephone. Obviously, they will want to talk to all involved in this operation, but right now I think you should call it a day. You look absolutely bushed. Go home to bed; write your report up later."

Proffitt got to his feet. "Yes, it has been a long night."

Chapter Twenty-Two

Detective Chief Inspector Richard Proffitt downed his fourth whisky – or was it his fifth, he was already losing count? – as he struggled to keep open his tired eyes. How much he would have preferred to be at home, looking for sleep rather than alcohol to bring him respite, however temporary, from his anguish, instead of propping up a bar in a half-empty lounge at Heathrow Airport.

There had been no surprise in receiving the summons to a meeting after such a disaster. What did surprise him was the sight of the figure that settled on a seat at an empty table. Those large, beautiful, blue, eyes, so alluringly full of promise, seductively flashing a greeting in his direction, could only belong to one person. He had never expected to see her again. Glass in hand, he moved across to join her.

"Well, this is a surprise, to say the least," he said, raising his glass in a mock toasting gesture and swallowing a large mouthful of the fiery liquid.

"It's not my usual line of work, as you well know," she agreed, taunting him with an arrogant smile. "So many people have already gone home for Christmas. There was no-one else to come."

"What shall I call you?" asked Proffitt. "Which name are you calling yourself today?"

"Whatever takes your fancy."

"What did Greenfield know you as?"

She paused to recollect. "Julie, I think. That's one of my favourites."

"Then Julie it will be." Again he raised his glass in mock salute. "In honour of the dear departed."

"Richard, you're drunk."

"Not drunk enough, unfortunately. Not yet."

"Men are so unbecoming when they are drunk." Her tone was now abrupt and angry. "I'm sure if they could see themselves, they wouldn't do it."

"I would rather not see myself at the moment, thank you." He stared down into his drink. "I don't want to see the blood on my hands."

"Don't be melodramatic, Richard." It could have been a schoolteacher admonishing a naughty child. "That's what the drink does for you."

Proffitt looked at this woman who sat across the table from him, unable to conceive how so much evil could manifest itself within so much beauty. It so often happened and it was one of nature's cruellest tricks. As her long sable coat fell casually open to reveal a beige woollen dress, drawn in at the waist by a narrow belt, so that it clung tightly against the shape of her body, it wasn't difficult to see why he and God knows how many others had fallen so easily under her spell. What man could resist those eyes? He hated her for what she was, yet just to see her and sit this closely to her was enough to arouse a degree of sensual intoxication within him.

It was she who broke the silence. "Richard, your masters are not pleased."

"No, it did turn out a bit of a mess, didn't it?"

"Why did you not tell us there was a surveillance detail?"

"There wasn't. Those officers were not under orders; they were acting on their own initiative. I told you who Tommy Morgan really was, didn't I?"

"That information was worth a lot of money to us. It also got us the elimination contract, so we are happy enough on that score. There is a feeling, however, you didn't go far enough."

"I didn't know you were going to take him out. I thought the information would lead to the bad guys pulling out and disappearing into the sunset. In any case, I didn't know two officers were going to follow him. There were four officers at the pub with me. I couldn't watch what all of them did or where they went after the operation had been called off for the night."

"How much is known?"

"Not a great deal. I don't think the weapon is going to reveal anything and Greenfield, himself, is a complete mystery. At the moment there's only one lead."

"The private investigator's report." Proffitt looked surprised, but Julie only smiled. "We helped write it and stopped the enquiries going any further. Have you seen it?"

"Yes, Greenfield's wife had it. I haven't told anybody yet, but I can't suppress it indefinitely. It doesn't say much, although it does mention you – by description, of course, not name. It could lead to some police investigations in Barcelona."

"We have covered our tracks. It would have attracted attention if we had blocked the private investigator's report completely, but we were in control of it. We have always had contingency plans for such a happening, but I don't think we expected to ever have to use them. Our methods had always proved so successful. No, it's more harmful to our reputation than anything else and that is bad. We can not advertise in our line of work obviously, we have to rely on word-of-mouth recommendation. Our reputation is everything to us."

The voice over the public address system announced a flight to Munich.

"That's my flight," said Julie. "I have to go now."

"Germany?"

"I am stopping with some friends over Christmas. When you have something to report, use the normal channels. Keep us up to date on this."

"No Julie." Proffitt spoke calmly, but resolutely. "I want out."

"That's impossible, Richard." She looked genuinely shocked. "A Detective Chief Inspector inside Scotland Yard, you're one of our prize assets. The information you have given us over the past three years has been worth a small fortune to us."

"Then settle for what I've given you, Julie. Let me have the film," he pleaded. "You've had three years of my life and now I have to live with the death of a dear friend and colleague on my conscience. I can't give you any more. You ask too much."

"Forget it, Richard, you're with us until the day you retire," she snapped, "unless you want your wife and kids, plus the whole of Scotland Yard, including the Commissioner, to see tapes of that film. We could probably get one to the Home Secretary too. Don't underestimate what we can do, not for a second."

"I can't go on." Proffitt's voice trembled as his alcoholic mood of melancholy tightened its grip. "I've seen too many widows' tears today."

Julie made no effort to conceal that her patience was close to being exhausted. "Today's tears will be yesterday's memories when you wake up tomorrow morning. Pull yourself together, Richard."

"You don't feel anything, do you?" Proffitt could eye her now with nothing but contempt. "No remorse, no compassion, not anything. How many times have you made love, Julie? Hundreds? How many hundreds? But I bet you've never loved. You don't know what feelings are."

"I weary of your sentimental rambling," she said coldly, showing no reaction to his analysis of her lack of sensitivity. "I really do have to go now."

"I have a gun, Julie."

She laughed out loud. "Really Richard, why don't you just go home and sleep it off? Even if you did have a gun, which I doubt, what would you hope to achieve by using it on me? Do you think I am the only one doing this sort of work?"

"You're the only one I know."

A further call for the Munich flight beamed out over the public address system.

"I must declare our little meeting closed," she said, gathering up her gloves and handbag.

Proffitt stared deeply into her eyes, searching in vain for a trace of emotion. "You can't even feel fear, can you? There's nothing there at all. You're an emotional zombie. You might as well be a robot."

Remaining unmoved, she replied in a brusque, matter-of-fact manner, "Call me names if it makes you happier, Richard, I can easily live with that, but you know well enough the consequences of harming me. You have too much to lose. You're not that stupid."

Proffitt watched her as she left the lounge, disappearing in the direction of passport control and the security checks, turning every male head as she passed. It was too easy for her. The thought depressed him further. Returning to the bar, he motioned for his glass to be refilled. Now he really had lost count.

As he sat on the bar stool the regulation issue .38 Smith and Wesson revolver, tucked into a holster attached to his belt, pressed against his hip. Weapons had been carried during the previous evening's operation at the Mole with Two Heads and, in the ensuing chaos of the night, he had simply overlooked turning his back in.

He found himself wondering if Mike Donovan's little boy had yet been told his Daddy was never coming home; not this Christmas or any other Christmas. The face of Donovan's widow – how swift was the transit from wife to widow, a fleeting moment in the passage of life – tear-stained, questioning, fearful, appeared before him, swirling around the remaining liquid in his glass, uttering over and over again, "Why, why, why?" The word reverberated around his brain, a never-fading echo. He shook his head violently and rubbed his eyes until tears welled up in them, but the image refused to go away.

They were being too greedy. If only they would release him now, let him have the film to destroy. Perhaps, in time, he could learn to live with the misery he had caused the previous night, but how many more would there be? How many more widows' tears was he going to have to face? The answer, he knew, was in his hands. The clock showed twenty-five minutes until the departure of the flight to Munich. He didn't finish his drink. He didn't need to. The decision had been easier than he expected.

How he wished he could turn back the clock. He had been assigned to help a police investigation in Kenya into the brutal murder of two British nationals working there. The Kenyan police had asked Scotland Yard for additional expertise and a team had been assembled, but Proffitt had been unable to travel with the other members due to a family commitment. It was a long flight and she was such good company, so charming, so attentive and so very beautiful. He knew he was not the best looking fellow in the world. A couple of inches under six feet, a body that looked somewhat overweight, despite his strength and general fitness, his thinning hair and premature bags beneath both eyes, he looked older than his forty-one years. Yet he was happily married and had a good home life, so had no reason to complain. However, having married his childhood sweetheart he had never been with another woman, so he had yielded to the temptation of the young, so beautiful woman who lavished so much attention on him. For him it was like a living dream, detached from the reality of his everyday life. A once-in-a-lifetime opportunity to stop the world and step off for a brief, but exciting, moment in time. What a price he had paid, yet regret was a hopeless emotion, borne only to make life's mistakes so much harder to survive.

His warrant card took him without query through the security check points, enabling him to by-pass the metal detectors that would have noisily revealed the presence of a weapon. There was no sign of her in the departure lounge. He prayed he was not too late. If she had already boarded the aircraft, his cause was lost.

He was only just in time, finding her almost at the front of the queue trickling through the boarding gate. A young, dark-haired woman, in airline uniform, stood collecting the boarding cards.

"Julie!"

The loud, bellowing cry of her name grabbed the attention of everyone in the queue. Julie's face froze with horror as she turned to look into the barrel of the revolver. Proffitt stood no more than ten yards away from her, legs slightly astride, the gun held out in front of him at eye level in both hands. There was a sudden burst of activity in the immediate vicinity as the queue scattered, people ducking and scurrying out of the line of fire, but Julie stood rooted by fear to the spot. Her long, piercing scream "Noooo!" was finally drowned out by the gunfire. The hands raised instinctively in front of her face were an impossible defence against the bullets that flew from the gun. Seeing the terror in her eyes, Proffitt's only feeling was that he had, at last, wrung an emotion from her.

Someone began to weep, someone quietly uttered what seemed to be a prayer, but most watched in stunned silence the tall man with the gun and the beautiful woman, the look of fear frozen rigidly on her face, lying on the floor, strangely in something resembling the foetal position, as her life's blood seeped out of the wounds in her throat and chest. First to move was the young woman in uniform, who had been standing closest to her. Initially screaming at the sound of the gunfire and the splattering of blood across her uniform and the side of her face as the bullets found their target, she quickly gathered her senses, summoning up the courage to kneel beside Julie, searching for signs of a pulse. Proffitt knew it was a hopeless gesture. A trained marksman, who practised every week without fail, his accuracy at that range was infallible.

He had no need to turn to know the meaning of the sound of running footsteps coming up behind him. Many times as a young, uniformed constable he had been assigned to airport duty at Heathrow. They were days of hope, high ideals and burning ambition, standing on the threshold of a career that now, nearly twenty years on, lay in ruins.

Prison life would be hard. It always was for an ex-policeman. He still had the gun in his hand. Put that in his mouth, a squeeze of the trigger, and it would all be over. He looked at the crumpled body on the floor. Even bloodied and in death she still looked so beautiful. How was that possible? To take his life would mean, in the final reckoning, she had won. That couldn't be allowed. He would take responsibility for his actions. In prison he would enjoy a degree of isolation from the public humiliation about to descend on his family. He had no doubt the threat to distribute the tapes would be carried out. His son and daughter were grown up, old enough and hopefully mature enough to cope with what they saw, however difficult it may be to understand why. The effect on his wife would be devastating, made worse by the prolonged and sensational media coverage it was certain to attract. He hoped she and his children would stand by him. God knows, he needed them now. Yet he had to admit it looked a forlorn hope and who could blame them?

"Armed police – put down your weapon."

Proffitt bent down slowly to place the weapon on the floor and kick it away from him.

"I'm a police officer. I know the drill."

He knelt down on the floor and then forward to lying face down, drawing his hands behind his back. Handcuffs were clamped tightly around his wrists, before he was hauled roughly to his feet.

"Please contact Commander Hawkes at Scotland Yard," instructed Proffitt firmly, staring into the barrels of the Heckler and Koch weaponry pointing menacingly at his head. "I wish to make a statement."

About the Author

I was born and raised in Birmingham, England, where I was educated at King Edward's Grammar School, Aston. I am married, with two grown-up daughters. A keen photographer, having had photographs published, I enjoy also cinema and theatre. A great follower of football or soccer as some call it, I am a long-time supporter of Birmingham-based professional club, Aston Villa, still regularly attending matches at their Villa Park home ground. Railways and especially the old steam locomotives are also a great interest, fortunately living in a country where this is a popular interest, so boasting a large number of heritage railways, one of the main ones not too far from where I live.

Although having spent most of my working life in financial environments, words, not figures, have always been my first love. I did spend some years as a freelance journalist, when I was local correspondent for a number of national trade magazines and worked some newspaper assignments. I have also worked in Press and Public Relations with a Birmingham-based advertising and public relations agency. My Penguin Books prize winning short story 'The Prisoner' was a prize winner in a competition organised jointly by Penguin Books and a local commercial radio station. I was interviewed on air and the story was broadcast, read by a leading actor from a popular daily national radio serial. Set in the early period of World War Two, the story revolved around a member of the Hitler Youth charged with returning an escaped prisoner from the occupied Channel Islands to the European mainland. It was also subsequently accepted for publication in 1992 in a short story book compilation 'Shorts from the Midlands.' More recently I made this story available free to read on the 'Authors Den' website, attracting more than 1,700 reads and favourable comments. Also, on this site is 'The Reluctant Father Christmas,' a Christmas short story I placed free to read two years ago, which has now clocked up more than 7,000 reads.

Other short stories have won prizes in minor competitions over the years and I have a number of short stories yet unpublished.

My crime thriller novel 'The Hit-and-Run Man,' published in 1991, may have been instrumental in stopping the U.K. cinema release of a Johnny Depp movie. The book hit the U.K. headlines in 1996, when, after reading Press previews of 'Nick of Time,' I raised concerns about notable similarities between the plot-lines of the movie and the book. Although not published in America, I was able to place the book as having been presented there, including a link with an agency claiming Hollywood connections. Not surprisingly, United International Pictures denied any knowledge of the book, but, despite favourable preview reviews, the movie was pulled from its U.K. cinema release and sent straight to video. In 2008 'The Hit-and-Run Man,' was a featured novel in the Four Counties Noir Festival - "A Festival of Crime Fiction from the Dark Heart of England" - at the Light House Media Centre, Wolverhampton, England and was selected for a reading.

The introduction of an IRA element into the novel is probably not a surprise as most of my life has been lived under a terrorist threat of some description and on two occasions has struck close to home. Although living a few miles outside Birmingham city centre I heard in the distance the explosions when in November 1974 IRA bombs exploded in two city centre public houses, killing 21 and injuring 182.

The second occasion was a more direct impact as I could have lost a close family member. In an incredible and almost fatal case of wrong time, wrong place, my brother, some three hundred miles from his home, was driving through Lockerbie when the bomb-shattered plane hit the ground. In the dark, he was aware of nothing until a huge explosion erupted ahead of him. His first instinct was that a petrol tanker had exploded and, indeed, it was probably escaping fuel that sent a fireball racing down the road towards the van he was driving. Rescue workers who found him wandering around dazed and in a severe state of shock were unsure who he was and even wondered at first if he was a plane survivor. Fortunately he must have reacted fast enough to avoid serious physical injury, though sustaining some burns to his face and scalp.

As an indie author I published a revised edition of the 'Hit-and-Run Man,' with additional material, as an e-book from Amazon Kindle in 2013.

Lightning Source UK Ltd.
Milton Keynes UK
UKHW011911121120
373303UK00001B/149